"You're Not Going To Believe Me, But When I Came Here Today, I Had No Intention Of Dragging You Off To Bed Like A Sex-Starved Caveman," He Said.

"'Kay."

"Are you angry?"

"Don't have the energy."

He chuckled and the sound _____ _____ _____ er ear. "Do you wan_____

She lifted her _____ "Sounds good."

"Since I interrup_____ _____er, why don't we shower togeth_____

"If my knees will hold me up."

He turned to his side, holding her in place against him. "Don't worry. I'll be there to catch you if you fall."

It was too late. She'd already fallen.

Dear Reader,

Why not make reading Silhouette Desire every month your New Year's resolution? It's a lot easier—and a heck of a lot more enjoyable—than diet or exercise!

We're starting 2006 off with a bang by launching a brand-new continuity: THE ELLIOTTS. The incomparable Leanne Banks gives us a glimpse into the lives of this high-powered Manhattan family, with *Billionaire's Proposition*. More stories about the Elliotts will follow every month throughout the year.

Also launching this month is Kathie DeNosky's trilogy, THE ILLEGITIMATE HEIRS. Three brothers born on the wrong side of the blanket learned they are destined for riches. The drama begins with *Engagement between Enemies*. *USA TODAY* bestselling author Annette Broadrick is back this month with *The Man Means Business*, a boss/secretary book with a tropical setting and a sensual story line.

Rounding out the month are great stories with heroes to suit your every mood. Roxanne St. Claire gives us a bad boy who needs to atone for *The Sins of His Past*. Michelle Celmer gives us a dedicated physical therapist who is not above making a few late-night *House Calls*. And Barbara Dunlop (who is new to Desire) brings us a sexy cowboy whose kiss is as shocking as a *Thunderbolt over Texas*.

Here's to keeping that New Year's resolution!

Melissa Jeglinski

Melissa Jeglinski
Senior Editor

Please address questions and book requests to:
Silhouette Reader Service
U.S.: 3010 Walden Ave., P.O. Box 1325, Buffalo, NY 14269
Canadian: P.O. Box 609, Fort Erie, Ont. L2A 5X3

ANNETTE BROADRICK

The Man Means Business

Published by Silhouette Books
America's Publisher of Contemporary Romance

SILHOUETTE BOOKS

ISBN 0-373-76701-3

THE MAN MEANS BUSINESS

This edition published by arrangement with Harlequin Books S.A.

® and TM are trademarks of Harlequin Books S.A., used under license.
Trademarks indicated with ® are registered in the United States Patent
and Trademark Office, the Canadian Trade Marks Office and in other
countries.

Visit Silhouette Books at www.eHarlequin.com

Printed in U.S.A.

Books by Annette Broadrick

Silhouette Desire

ANNETTE BROADRICK

believes in romance and the magic of life. Since 1984, Annette has shared her view of life and love with readers. In addition to being nominated by *Romantic Times BOOKclub* as one of the Best New Authors of that year, she has also won the *Romantic Times BOOKclub* Reviewers' Choice Award for Best in its Series; the *Romantic Times BOOKclub* WISH Award; and the *Romantic Times BOOKclub* Lifetime Achievement Awards for Series Romance and Series Romantic Fantasy.

To Ralph and Betty Carruthers, who believe that family comes first, for which I'm extremely grateful.

One

"**M**an your battle stations! Incoming! Incoming!"

Jodie Cameron grinned at the innovative way the receptionist notified her that the man she worked for had finally arrived at the office on this gloomy winter day in Chicago.

"Thanks, Betty." Jodie cleared her computer screen, brushed a wisp of hair that had escaped the tidy knot at the back of her neck away from her face and waited for him.

Jodie knew something was up with Dean Logan. In the five years she'd worked for him Dean had never come to work this late in the morning. He generally was already there when she arrived.

Earlier she'd checked his calendar to see if he was scheduled to go out of town, but he had nothing written down. She had wondered if he'd decided not to come in since it was Friday and he planned to go on a week's vacation starting on Sunday. But that didn't seem likely. He would have called to let her know.

This would be the first vacation he'd taken since she'd been his secretary, and she looked forward to having the time to clean out files, set up subfiles and work uninterrupted.

At least Betty had warned her that he wasn't in the best of moods. Dean was moody at the best of times, but no matter how cranky he was this morning, she could put up with him for one more day.

She waited at her desk for him to enter her office.

Dean was an astute businessman and he'd worked hard to build his electronic security business. She had no idea why he didn't appear content with what he'd accomplished during the past fifteen years.

The man looked more like a football player than the head of a multimillion-dollar corporation. Too bad he rarely smiled. As far as she could recall, she'd never heard him laugh.

He was not the jovial type.

His face looked as if it had been carved out of granite and his nose had been broken at some point. His heavy brows and piercing silver-blue eyes would never get him selected to a list of America's sexiest bachelors.

Not that his looks stopped the bevy of beauties who flocked around him. Each hoped to have the distinction of becoming Mrs. Dean Logan.

From what Jodie could tell, he neither encouraged them nor discouraged them. Rachel Hunt was his latest arm candy. He'd been seeing her for almost three months now, which was close to a record for him.

Jodie knew when he started seeing someone new because he had her take care of sending flowers, ordering gifts, obtaining tickets for various events and, at times, listening to his comments about the women who came and went in his life.

He knew that most of the women were more interested in his money and connections than in him. He listened cynically to confessions of undying love and a yearning for a commitment he refused to give.

Hence the number of women who came in and out of his life.

There were times when Jodie saw the loneliness in his eyes. At some point, long before she'd come to work for him, Dean must have made the decision not to allow anyone to get close to him. She found that to be very sad. Not that she'd ever let him know that she pitied him. No, she listened when he needed to talk and kept her opinions to herself.

Of course, her sister would never believe that, since Jodie was known for expressing her opinion on myriad subjects at any given moment. She smiled at the thought.

Dean moved silently, and she had grown used to his suddenly appearing in her doorway. As he did now.

"Good morn—"

"No, it definitely is not a good morning." Dean stopped in front of her desk, pulled an envelope out of his coat pocket and handed it to her. "I won't need these." He started into his office. "Would you mind getting me some coffee, please? I have a hellacious headache."

"Sure," she replied absently. She picked up the envelope and looked inside. The envelope held the airline tickets to Hawaii that she'd ordered for Dean and Rachel. Had Rachel changed her mind about going?

She stood and walked over to the coffeepot, filled one of the large mugs she kept nearby and followed him into his office.

Dean stood with his hands in his pockets looking out the window. She set the cup on his desk and sat in her usual chair.

"What happened, Dean?"

He didn't answer right away. Instead he stared out at the spitting snow and occasional ice blowing against the glass. She waited.

After several minutes of silence, he turned and sat down behind his desk, reaching for the coffee. "Do you have any aspirin?"

"Certainly." She went to the small bar behind a sliding door and poured him a glass of water before she picked up the aspirin bottle and set it in front of him.

He really was in a ferocious mood. His frown, always intimidating, was firmly in place. No wonder people were wary of him. She didn't think he realized how gruff he sounded...and that was on one of his good days.

When she'd first gone to work for him, Jodie knew she had replaced a string of four women who had attempted to work for him and left after only a few weeks. So she'd been warned.

However, she was made of sterner stuff. She'd been raised with three brothers and she and her sister had learned to hold their own with the boys.

After several minutes of silence, Dean looked at her with a puzzled expression. "Why are you here?"

"I work here," she replied with a straight face.

He closed his eyes. "Sorry. I'm not in the best of moods."

No kidding. And he'd actually apologized! She must mark the day on her calendar.

"How long have you worked for me?"

"Five years."

"Why?"

"Why what?"

"If I'm such a disagreeable person, why do you put up with me?"

"Who said you're a disagreeable person? I find you extremely agreeable as long as you get your own way," she replied lightly.

"Rachel says that everyone in this office is intimidated by me. But you aren't."

"I wasn't aware that was part of my job description. Is that what's bothering you this morning?"

"No."

"Do you care what people in the office think of you?"

"No. Well, except for you. What do you think of me?"

She sat back in her chair and considered her answer. Finally she looked him in the eye and said, "I think you're a brilliant man who is impatient with people, a man who has single-handedly built this company into a thriving corporation by ignoring the naysayers and following your own vision."

"Hmph."

He took the aspirin and drank the water. Then he picked up his coffee and sipped.

They sat in silence for several more minutes.

Finally Dean said, "Rachel broke up with me last night."

She couldn't hide her surprise. That must be a first for Dean. He was generally the one who broke things off any time a woman wanted more from him than he was willing to offer.

"Because you wanted her to go to Hawaii with you?" she asked, her disbelief plain.

He grimaced. "Actually she didn't give me a chance to surprise her with the tickets before she informed me that she never wanted to see me again."

Jodie was caught off guard by his admission. "Oh? I didn't realize you'd planned the trip as a surprise."

"Well, I did. Turns out I was the one surprised."

"What in the world happened?"

"I forgot we had tickets to the opera last night. I worked late to clear my desk and I'd forgotten to put the opera on my calendar."

"Oops."

"By the time I checked my cell phone messages on the way home, I was an hour late picking her up."

"Uh-oh."

"She was furious when I arrived at her place. I pointed out that we could still get there before intermission. It wasn't as if we didn't know the story, after all. However, the opera no longer mattered as far as she was concerned." He scrubbed his face with his hand. "She handed me a sack with the things I'd left in her apartment since we've been seeing each other and told me to get out."

"Rachel was obviously upset at the time," Jodie said. "Why don't you call her today and tell her about the trip you've planned? I'm sure you'll be back in her good graces once she discovers your surprise."

He was shaking his head before she finished. "I'm not going to do that. She made it plain she wanted no part of me, so why should I bother?" His mouth turned up at the corners. "I'll admit my ego might have been bruised a little and I went home to sulk, but she made it clear that we were through. I can accept that."

He nodded toward the envelope she'd placed on his desk. "So," he said with a shrug, "I won't be needing those."

Oh, dear. She'd promised herself never to offer her opinion unless he asked for it—and then any question he asked invariably had to do with business.

She wrestled with her conscience for a long moment but could no longer remain quiet. "I disagree," she said bravely, bracing for his response. "I believe you need the time away whether Rachel is with you or not. You know you love Hawaii and it's been three years since you acquired the condo there. I think you should go and spend some time on the beach. Forget the business for a few days. Catch up on your sleep. Once you're there, I know you'll enjoy it."

He leaned back in his chair and stared at her. She waited for his salvo telling her to mind her own business. Jodie was surprised when instead he asked, "Do you think I'm married to my job?"

She eyed him uncertainly. This man had never questioned himself in front of her before. Now that he'd asked her opinion, she wondered how candid she could be while he was in this unusual mood. "Maybe," she said cautiously.

He lowered his brows and stared at her. "Gee, thanks."

She might as well continue. "Look at it this way. You needed to put in long hours when you first started the company and you got into the habit of spending most of your time here. Now you've hired people you can rely on to take care of the day-to-day business. Maybe it's time for you to discover other things you might like to do with your life besides work."

He rubbed his chin. "I suppose." He shook his head. "I still can't get over how angry Rachel was when I arrived. What did I do that was so bad, please tell me? She could have called a cab when she couldn't reach me and been able to see the whole thing."

"Did you by any chance call her after you listened to her messages?"

"Why? I was on my way to pick her up by that time."

She coughed to hide her amusement. "My guess is that her irritation was the result of an accumulation of times when you've been late or forgotten to call or gone out of town without notice. Some women can find that sort of behavior off-putting."

"You don't."

"You pay me quite well not to notice. Besides, I'm your secretary, not your girlfriend."

He studied her in silence for a moment. "That's only going to last another few months," he said, not sounding at all pleased. "You'll be moving over to Frank's department in June."

She grinned. "All thanks to you."

"You caught me in a rare moment of gratitude for your hard work. You graduate with your degree in business this spring, don't you?"

"That's right. I wouldn't have been able to take the night classes without your paying for my tuition."

"I didn't pay it," he growled. "The company did. It was strictly a sound business decision. With your knowledge of the company and your quick grasp of things, it would be foolish to hold you back from exercising your full potential."

He rubbed his forehead as though the headache was hanging on. "Of course, that means I'll go through hell finding someone to work for me."

"No, you won't. I'll do the screening. If I think some-one—male or female—will be able to work with you without running the first time you raise your voice, I'll set up an appointment for you to meet them."

"I suppose that might work." He didn't look happy at the thought.

His decision to promote her had been quite a sacrifice for him and she knew it. Beneath that tough, gruff exterior was a very fair man.

Of course, he was clueless about women, but what man wasn't?

"Do you socialize much?" he asked, surprising her again. He'd never shown any interest in her personal life. He was definitely in a strange mood today.

"I date occasionally. Of course, going to school three nights a week and studying takes up most of my spare time."

"I work you too hard."

She offered him a cheerful smile. "Comes with the territory."

"The only reason I planned the trip was to appease Rachel, even if I was a little late in doing so. However, there is a man I'd like to meet in Honolulu. Steve Furukawa owns several businesses in the islands, and I'd like to offer our services to him." He studied her for a moment. "In case he's interested, I'd need you to help me make a presentation to him. I think we should both fly out there. We'll spend a day or two on business and the rest of the time we'll be on vacation."

"Me?" She almost strangled on the word. "I can't do something like that!"

"Why not?"

She stared at him in disbelief. Didn't he understand? Obviously not.

"I'm in the middle of classes, for one thing. And it just doesn't look right, our going to Hawaii together."

"It will be a business trip."

"You've never needed me on one before."

"Jodie, you're a very competent secretary and level-headed. As for school, I doubt missing a week's worth of classes will cause you to flunk. Will it?"

"Well, no, but—"

"Then I don't see a problem." He ruffled through the stack of files on his desk. "Would you check with accounting and see if they have the latest figures on the Malone file? I'd like to see them before lunch if possible."

Two

"**W**hat did you say to him?" Jodie's sister, Lynette, asked her that evening after dinner.

Jodie had a standing invitation for dinner at Chuck and Lynette's home every Friday, but she'd never had such earthshaking news to share as she did tonight.

Chuck had called earlier to say he'd be home later than normal and for them not to hold dinner for him. Jodie hadn't mentioned Dean's plan when she'd arrived. Instead she'd helped with dinner and then made certain that her nephews, Kent and Kyle—seven and six respectively—got their baths and were ready for bed.

It was only after she'd joined Lynette in the living room while she nursed eight-week-old Emily that Jodie dropped her bombshell.

"I think I muttered something but don't remember what. I was reeling."

"You're going, of course."

"He practically ordered me to go," Jodie wailed with a laugh.

"When are you supposed to leave?"

"The tickets are for Sunday morning. Early Sunday morning."

"So his latest darling finally had enough of your romantically challenged boss, did she? She lasted longer than the others, though."

"I think what got to him was that she was the one who broke things off. He usually has the privilege of doing that. At least he got a taste of what rejection feels like."

"I can't believe she turned down a trip to Hawaii. I would have gone and then broken up with him," Lynette said with a grin.

"She didn't know about his plans. He'd kept the trip a surprise."

Lynette shook her head with disbelief. "Doesn't the man know anything about women? The anticipation of going is part of the excitement."

"We're talking about Dean Logan. Of course he doesn't know anything about us. For a brilliant businessman, he's unnervingly obtuse about the opposite sex."

"Well, who cares, if you get a free vacation out of it?"

"I'll be missing three classes."

"So? You've aced all your tests, you can easily catch up."

The door opened between the garage and kitchen, and Lynette peered over her shoulder. Chuck was home.

"Good evening, all," he said, sauntering into the room.

He was a police detective for the city and looked good in his sports jacket and slacks. "How are my three favorite women doing?" He leaned over Lynette and gave her a leisurely kiss that made Jodie's toes curl to watch.

When he straightened, he brushed his lips across the top of Emily's head. Emily ignored him. Dinner was more important at the moment.

"Your dinner's in the fridge. Just put it in the microwave."

"How are things going for you, Jodie?" he asked casually as he turned to go back into the kitchen.

Before Jodie had a chance to answer, Lynette said, "Her boss has invited her to go with him to Hawaii for a week."

Chuck stopped in his tracks and spun around. "Are you serious? Logan asked you to go away with him? Wow. Aren't you the sly one? I had no idea you two were an item."

"We're not! Believe me, there is nothing going on in a romantic sense. The girl he's been seeing broke up with him. He had the tickets. I suggested he should take the vacation anyway, and he decided to meet with a prospective client while he was there. He said he could use my help. So it will be a working vacation."

Chuck grinned. "And you believed him."

"Of course. Why shouldn't I?"

Chuck, his dinner forgotten, sat down next to Lynette. "Jodie. Honey. Let's get real, okay? A man doesn't invite his good-looking secretary to go away with him to a tropical isle without some strictly male motive. He's going to do his best to get you into his bed. Count on it."

"Chuck!" Lynette kept her voice soft but emphatic. Jodie wondered how she did that. "Not every man has sex on the brain like you do."

He gave her an intimate smile. "Oh, yes, they do. Some just hide it better than others."

Jodie said, "You're probably right, Chuck, but Dean is a definite exception. I've worked for him too many years not to know that he doesn't notice me as a woman. I'm an efficient machine to him and that's fine with me."

"If you say so. When do you leave?"

"Sunday morning."

"Have you ever been to Hawaii?"

"No."

"Then go and enjoy yourself. I would guess he's picking up the tab for your accommodations."

"Actually he acquired a condo there a few years ago. It was part of a business deal he made. He went over to check it out and that's the last time he was there. There are three bedrooms and three baths. I think the company he bought it from used the condo for the executives to, quote, get away, unquote, for some relaxation."

"So he'll have you right where he wants you for a leisurely seduction," Chuck replied, twisting his imaginary mustache with a grin.

"Nothing wrong with your imagination, that's for sure," Jodie replied, laughing. "If you'd ever met him, you'd see how far off base you are."

"Why? Is he some kind of monster?"

"Let's just say he takes some getting used to. Once his business is completed he'll probably forget that I'm there."

Lynette said, "Now that's carrying the platonic bit too far, sis. There's bound to be a middle ground between what you've imagined and what my crazy husband came up with."

"So you two think I should go ahead and plan to go?"

They answered in unison. "Yes."

"But what about the talk around the office?" Jodie asked. " Won't that give everyone the wrong idea?"

"So what?" Chuck answered. "It will give them something to gossip about. Probably improve morale. The office employees will start a betting pool as to when you'll announce your engagement."

"You're a big help," Lynette said, shaking her head at her spouse. "The idea here is to give her reasons to go, not make up stuff."

"Well, since it looks as though I'm going, I'll need to go shopping for beachwear tomorrow."

"Great idea. Buy some things that are colorful and tropical. No business suits." She eyed her for a moment. "You've said you never have time to get your hair cut. Why don't you get it trimmed tomorrow, as well?"

Jodie nodded. "I could do that."

"And get plenty of sunscreen. You know how easily we burn, thanks to our Scandinavian ancestors."

Jodie looked at her arms and ruefully shook her head. "I hope to come back with at least a little more color. I'll slather myself with the stuff and see what happens."

Lynette lifted Emily to her shoulder and rubbed her back until she gave a very unladylike belch, causing the three of them to laugh. "I need to put her down," Lynette said. "I'll be right back."

"I need to go, you guys. It's been a long week," Jodie said, rising. "And it looks like I'll be spending tomorrow shopping."

"Poor baby," Lynette consoled with a grin. "That's your favorite hobby in the entire world, and we both know it."

"True. And buying summer things in the dead of winter will be just the thing I need to get into the spirit of the trip."

Later that night while Jodie prepared for bed, she thought about the comments she'd heard tonight from Lynette and Chuck. She scrubbed her teeth and removed her makeup before looking in the mirror.

"Are you going to be brave and treat this as a chance in a lifetime to see Hawaii with all expenses paid?"

Here image stared back at her with sparkling eyes.

After a long pause, she sighed and said, "You're no help. You want to see Hawaii. Will the trade-off be worth it? Hawaii with all its pleasures weighed against a week with a man who's a workaholic? Knowing Dean, he'll have us working the whole time we're there.

Then again, we're bound to find some time to enjoy the sun and sand.

She smiled as she crawled into bed.

Three

Dean stood in front of the mirror shaving early Sunday morning and wondered what he was doing. Had he lost his mind?

What had possessed him to invite his secretary to go with him to Hawaii? She was a great secretary. In fact, she was a great human being, but he didn't need to spend a week with her to be reminded of the fact.

Of course, if he planned to meet with Furukawa, he could use her presence there to help him make a presentation and to help formulate a contract. She was very conscientious and did her work without a complaint.

But to take her to Hawaii with him?

Had his midlife crisis arrived sooner than expected? Why else would he have considered taking her? He knew nothing about her outside of the office. Well, he knew she was single, but that was about it. Did she have family close by? Would they warn her about going with him?

He could get in trouble for harassment.

Well. Maybe that was a little extreme. She'd had the option to say no. When he'd called her at home last night she'd sounded agreeable enough. He certainly hadn't coerced her. At least, not much.

He finished dressing and picked up the bag he'd packed. He'd had trouble knowing what to pack besides his business clothes. The only other time he'd been there, his business suits had been expected, but then he hadn't been on vacation. He'd spent the three days in meetings, ironing out the conditions of the merger with the parties involved.

He'd tossed in a few shirts and khaki pants this morning and even remembered to stick in a pair of tennis shoes, which was a laugh. He hadn't played tennis in years, but it was the idea that counted.

Maybe he *was* a little too focused on business. Working hard had become a habit, and he wasn't certain that he could break it.

Or that he wanted to.

He'd really let Rachel's comments get to him, which was ridiculous. What did he care what she thought about him? He'd just been surprised, that's all.

He and Jodie would get along well enough for the few days they'd be there, he was fairly certain. He'd treat the trip as a bonus for Jodie in appreciation for her years of service.

He smiled at the thought, pleased that he'd found the correct category for the trip.

* * *

Jodie had almost reached the door into the airport before Dean recognized her. She looked different, but why? Then he realized that she was wearing her hair down. He'd never seen her wear it any way but pulled back into a knot on the nape of her neck. It danced around her neck and shoulders in the wind. She certainly looked different this morning.

He glanced at his watch and frowned.

As soon as Jodie stepped out of the cab, she spotted Dean waiting for her just inside the door to the airline check-in counters. She hurriedly crossed the sidewalk toward him.

The wind-chill factor must be in the teens. Hawaii sounded better and better to her. At least she'd be getting away from the wonderful winter weather of dear old Chicago for a few days. She looked forward to soaking up some sun.

Just as she reached the door, he opened it and took her bag. "You're late," he snapped. "Security is tight and I don't want to miss the flight."

Actually she was forty-five minutes earlier than the airline recommended, but she wasn't going to start their trip together disputing his words. Instead she smiled at him and said, "I'm here now and good morning to you. Have you checked your luggage?"

"Yes." He glanced down at her suitcase. "Is this all you're taking?"

She looked down at her bag and then back up at him. "We're only going to be gone a week," she replied.

"I thought women packed three or four suitcases wherever they went," he mumbled.

"Not me."

"Well," he said awkwardly. "That's good."

She walked over to join the line to the counter and he followed her. "I might as well stay with you. No sense losing you in this crowd."

Jodie realized that he was nervous! She found that hard to believe, considering how much traveling he did. Was it because she was along?

She hadn't spotted it at first, probably because she'd been shaken by his accusation that she may have caused them to miss their plane. There was no way she would lose him in the crowd. As tall as he was, she'd spot him in any group.

She circumspectly checked out what he'd chosen to wear for the trip and was pleasantly surprised to see him in black pants, a black turtleneck sweater and a black leather jacket that fit snugly at his waist.

The wind had ruffled his dark hair and the leather jacket made him appear dangerous and very masculine.

He looked downright swashbuckling.

Now if he'd only smile once in a while, he could be attractive.

They reached their plane with time to spare, which Jodie wisely did not point out. Dean stopped and bought himself a paper and a couple of magazines. Jodie found the newest book out by one of her favorite authors, as well as a crossword puzzle book in case she got tired of reading.

She watched Dean as he paced the concourse. Was the man ever still? She placed her parka on her lap and started reading.

When it was time to board, first-class passengers were seated first. Not too bad. Dean waved her to the window seat before settling down beside her. A flight attendant checked to see what they would like to drink and handed them menus for breakfast.

Once they gave their orders, Jodie settled comfortably into the luxurious depths of her seat and looked around her.

The only time she'd seen first class on her flights was when she'd walked through to the tourist section. What a way to travel.

"Are you nervous about flying?" he asked after several minutes of silence.

She'd been peering out the window when he asked, and she straightened. "A little perhaps. Why?"

"I noticed your fingers gripping the armrests, and the plane hasn't moved."

She jerked her hands away and folded them into her lap. After a moment she dug into her purse and pulled out the book she'd been reading but gave up a few minutes later because she couldn't seem to concentrate. Maybe she'd work one of the crossword puzzles.

After another prolonged silence—were they ever going to leave the terminal?—Jodie asked, "How long is the flight, do you recall? I've forgotten what the reservations said."

"About thirteen hours, depending on a headwind. We change planes in Los Angeles."

"Oh."

"We should reach Maui by midafternoon local time."

"But we'll still be on Midwest time."

"True."

Well, she'd exhausted all her skills at social chitchat

with him. Jodie picked up the airline magazine and began to thumb through it.

After what felt like hours, the plane finally taxied out to the runway for takeoff. Then it stopped. The captain apologized for the delay. There were nine jets ahead of this one. Great. That gave her plenty of time to rethink this whole idea.

Dean cleared his throat. "Jodie?"

She'd just peered out the window again. "Yes?"

"I'm a little embarrassed to mention this after you've worked for me so many years, but I really don't know much about you besides your work ethic, which is outstanding, and your determination to get your degree, which is admirable. I'd like to learn more about you. Why don't we use this time to get acquainted?"

"I'm sorry, but I really don't want to talk right now. I need all my concentration once we're ready for takeoff to make absolutely certain the plane's wings are firmly attached." After all, there was a lot of thrust by the jet engines, and everyone knew that takeoffs and landings were the most dangerous times during a flight. Unless they happened to fly into the side of a mountain. They had to cross the Rockies, didn't they?

Or if they went down over water…say, maybe the Pacific Ocean?

"Jodie?" She jerked her head away from the window and looked at him inquiringly.

"We're perfectly safe, you know."

"Of course we are," she promptly agreed. "As long as we sit here on the runway." She glanced back out the window to continue to check the wings.

Dean made some kind of noise that sounded as if he was either choking or coughing. She looked back at him in concern. His lips were compressed and he wore a frown. His shoulders shook and suddenly, like Mount St. Helens, he erupted into laughter.

Laughter? She had rarely seen him smile, much less heard him laugh, and she stared at him in amazement. What a difference it made in him. He looked much younger than his thirty-eight years. Who would have believed it?

He immediately attempted to quell the sound, but then he looked at her again, recognized her bemusement, shook his head and continued to laugh—a deep-throated sound that finally made her smile.

He reached for his handkerchief and wiped his eyes, blew his nose and finally, after what seemed like forever, managed to stop.

But he continued to smile and she still hadn't recovered from the change in him. Dean was smiling and, miracle of miracles, his face hadn't cracked into a thousand little pieces. Who would have believed it?

"Care to share the joke?" she asked. She smiled her pleasure at this unexpected peek into the man she thought she knew so well.

He touched her arm and slid his hand down, lacing his fingers between hers. "I'm sorry. I shouldn't have laughed at your nervousness. You're going to be just fine, I promise."

"From your lips to God's ear," she muttered.

He chuckled again. He was certainly getting a great deal of amusement out of her fear of flying. Then again, maybe it was worth it to see that the man had a human side. A decidedly masculine side at that.

The brackets around his mouth had revealed dimples. She bet he hated them.

In fact, the man bore little resemblance to her stone-faced boss. Same hair and eyes, same strong jaw, and yet with his silver-blue eyes sparkling and his teeth flashing he was actually handsome.

Okay, she was losing it. When she looked at Dean Logan and saw a handsome man she knew she'd lost her grip. Fear could certainly do crazy things to a person's perceptions.

"I was born in Indiana," he said in a casual voice as though answering her question. "Came to Chicago to attend Northwestern and never left. How about you?"

She cleared her throat. "We're from Wisconsin originally."

"Who is we?"

"Mom, my three brothers, my sister and me. My parents got married way too young, but they were in love and didn't want to wait until after they finished school to get married. My brother came along not long afterward, and Dad dropped out of college to get a job. He took good care of all of us, but I think he pushed himself too hard for too many years and he died of a heart attack when he was forty-five.

"Mom had to get a job but had trouble finding one since she'd never worked before. Without training or an education, it was tough going for her. She ended up as a waitress. Both Mom and Dad really stressed the importance of an education when we were growing up. All three of my brothers worked their way through college so they could take care of her."

"Where does your family live?"

"All over the place. Mom's in Phoenix. That's where

they lived when Dad died. One of my brothers is an attorney in Oregon, one is career Navy and based out of Bremerton, Washington, and one lives just outside of D.C. doing who knows what. If anyone asks, he says, 'I work for the government' in a vague way and changes the subject. My sister, Lynette, and I live here in Chicago."

"Do any of them have children?"

She smiled. "Chuck and Lynette have two boys and a brand-new baby girl. The boys are pleased as little boys can be that they have a baby sister. My sister had two miscarriages before Emily came along."

"Are any of your brothers married?"

"Not a one. Too busy with work or too busy playing the field." She waited, and when he didn't ask any more questions, she said, "It's your turn. Tell me about your family."

She wasn't sure at first that he was going to answer her, but eventually he said, "My mother lives in a nursing home here. I had an older brother, but he and my dad were out on Lake Michigan at the wrong time years ago. A storm blew up and they didn't make it back."

"How awful. How old was your brother?"

"Twelve. I was eight and had a cold, so my mother wouldn't let me go with them." He looked away. After two or three minutes he added, "I haven't talked about them in years."

She wondered about the emotional scars he carried from that time. No doubt he'd been upset, probably angry, that he didn't get to go. Then to lose them like that. Survivor's guilt probably played a part. She knew him well enough not to say any more by way of sympathy for his loss.

"Why aren't you married?" he asked bluntly.

She looked at him in surprise. "Isn't that a rather personal question to ask?"

"Probably. But if I'm going to drag out all my personal stuff, I figure you can, too."

"Mmm. I don't think it's quite the same, unless you want to discuss why *you're* not married."

"That's easy enough. I have no intention of getting married. I was engaged once, but she found someone who had more money and broke the engagement six weeks before the wedding." He shrugged. "She's on her third marriage now, so she did me a favor. After that I decided to devote my time and energy to building my business, which was much more important to me than getting too involved in a relationship."

"You know, Dean, one of these days you're going to meet the woman you've been waiting for your whole life. And when you do, you'll be a goner."

"Somehow I doubt that very much." He studied her for a moment in silence. "So," he finally said, "have you ever been married?"

She shook her head, feeling a little exasperated with him. His persistence was one of his strongest traits. It made him an excellent businessman. But she didn't particularly like it when he aimed his curiosity at her.

Before she could decide how much she wanted to share with him, the captain's voice came over the speakers and said they were next to take off.

She immediately tightened her seat belt.

"Any tighter and you'll cut off the blood flow to the rest of your body," he said drily.

She took a deep breath, held it briefly and slowly exhaled. She was being an idiot. She adjusted the strap around her and forcibly relaxed her shoulders.

"No," she finally said in a strained voice. "I have never been married."

"Why not?"

"Because I haven't wanted to be, obviously."

"Any particular reason?"

"I feel like you have me under a microscope."

"Why? We're going to be together for the next week. I just want to get to know who you are when you're away from the office."

"Oh, all right. I had one serious relationship when I was nineteen. I shared a tiny apartment with one of my co-workers. We were both secretaries in a law firm and that's where I met him. He was a law student working at the firm part-time.

"We dated for more than a year and we talked about marriage once he finished law school. We spent most of our free time together. Everything was perfect…until I came home early one night and found him in bed with my roommate."

"Ouch."

"Yeah."

"Did he explain why?"

"To hear him tell it, he'd left school early and thought I might be home. When I wasn't, my roommate suggested he wait there for me. I'm sure she planned everything to work out the way it did. His explanation was that she was there and one thing led to another and it didn't mean anything. He apologized. Said it would never happen again."

"And you said?"

"I was very dignified. I told him if he ever made an attempt to see me again, I'd severely injure a delicate part of his anatomy."

He made a strangling sound but didn't comment.

"He pretty much left me alone after that. He and my ex-friend/roommate got married a few months later because she was pregnant. I don't know what happened after that because I accepted the job I have now and moved closer to work."

"You took it hard."

"That I did. There's something about finding out that someone you considered a friend and the man you thought you were going to marry betrayed you that dampens the spirit."

"But that was—what?—five years ago?"

"About that."

"And you haven't had a relationship since?"

"Not a serious one, no," she said, knowing she sounded defensive. "I just don't intend to get hurt again. So I don't allow anyone to get too close."

He looked at their hands, still entwined. "Then I feel honored."

She lowered her brows and glared at him. "We are not close. I work for you. Just because you think I'll try to get out of this plane before we take off doesn't mean we're close." She pulled her hand away just as the plane began to roll.

"Actually you work for the company."

"You are the company. Like I said, I work for you." Faking nonchalance, she picked up the book and determinedly began to read, hoping his questions were at an end.

Four

Jodie was glad to get off the plane in Los Angeles and walk around. She'd finished her book and decided to get more reading material.

"We have time to get something to eat if you'd like," Dean said as they walked past several small restaurants located along the concourse.

"I'm not really hungry. They'll feed us on this next flight, won't they?"

"Yes."

"Then I'll wait."

She glanced out the glass walls and saw sunshine, blue skies and palm trees. What a difference from Chicago. "I've never been to L.A. before. I guess this doesn't count since all I'm seeing is the airport."

"Don't you like to travel?" he asked. He motioned for her to go into one of the coffee shops with him.

"I haven't done all that much. I've flown to Phoenix several times to see my mother. One Christmas the family gathered in Oregon at my brother's place. Otherwise, my schedule keeps me too busy."

They got their coffee and found a small table near the glass wall overlooking one of the runways. "Then I'm glad you've come with me this week."

"Thank you."

"I hope this isn't out of line, but I can't get over how different you look with your hair down."

"Ah. You have no problem asking why I'm not married but hesitate to make a comment about my hair?"

"You have a point. Is it too late to apologize for my earlier questions?"

"Much too late since you listened to the entire tawdry story." She spoiled her solemn reprimand by chuckling at the expression on his face. "Do you like my hair shorter?"

"Oh. You had it cut."

"Yesterday." She ran her fingers through it. "I'm still getting used to it myself."

"It's, uh, you look very, uh—" He stopped. "Yes, I like it."

"Why, thank you." She looked around them. "Are you ready to find the gate for the next leg of our trip?"

He stood and stretched, briefly causing a gap between his sweater and pants. His stomach was flat and toned. She wondered what he'd look like in a bathing suit.

On the way to the gate Jodie picked up a couple of magazines. She was a little more relaxed for this second flight.

In fact, she was getting sleepy despite the coffee. Perhaps she'd be able to nap once they got into the air.

Jodie stirred as the captain announced that the plane would be making its descent into Kahului Airport, Maui, and that they would be landing in forty minutes.

She couldn't believe she'd slept that long. She glanced at her lap and saw the magazine she'd been reading when she'd fallen asleep.

She looked over at Dean. He wore his horn-rimmed reading glasses and seemed engrossed in a technical manual. No murder mysteries and thrillers for that man.

"I see you found something light and entertaining for your vacation reading," she said.

He lowered his chin and looked over his glasses at her. "Each of us relaxes in his own way. Did you sleep okay?"

"Surprisingly so." She covered her mouth and yawned. "I could get used to traveling in style." She waited a beat and said, "If you'll excuse me, I'd like to go freshen up before the seat-belt light comes on."

Dean moved promptly out of his chair and stepped back. She walked to the front and saw that the lavatory was unoccupied, thank goodness. She went in and locked the door. After she washed her hands, she found her comb and ran it through her hair.

The haircut really did give her a different look. The waves fell around her face and called attention to her eyes. She was surprised that Dean had not only noticed but commented on her appearance.

She felt that she'd been on the plane for at least a week and wondered if she'd ever get the constant drone of the engines out of her head. When she opened the door, she found another first-class passenger standing there. She smiled. He returned her smile with interest.

Jodie felt herself blush and hurriedly returned to her seat. Dean had seen her coming and was standing in the aisle out of her way when she arrived.

"Thank you," she said hurriedly and slipped into her seat.

He sat down beside her and closed the manual he'd been reading.

During the next fifteen minutes he asked her a few more questions about her life—her hobbies, favorite movies and television shows—and she gave him brief answers, at least enough to satisfy him. After that he left her to read her magazine.

She still felt strange about traveling with him, but she'd no doubt get over that once they arrived at the condo and she set up a routine of sorts.

Once they landed, she and Dean methodically checked around them for their belongings before getting off the plane. Anyone seeing them would think they were a couple who'd been married for years. She had no idea why the thought made her nervous.

Once in the terminal, Jodie noticed that many of the people on departing flights wore leis. She smiled, looking forward to getting one for herself. Dean found an available taxi and he and the driver put their bags in the trunk of the cab.

Dean settled into the seat next to her. "So what do you think?"

"I'm amazed. The scented air is refreshing."

"Beats the heck out of car exhausts and diesel fuel."

She glanced at Dean while he gazed out the window and asked questions of the driver. He already looked more relaxed than she'd ever seen him. That was good. She had hopes that the rest would do him good.

The scenery was breathtaking, with towering mountains on one side and the ocean on the other. They followed the coast for several miles until the taxi slowed and turned onto a lane that led to security gates.

Dean gave his name and the gates swung open.

Once inside the gated area, the lane wound through tropical foliage that looked green and lush. When they reached the building, she felt that they'd burst into sunshine with a panoramic view of the sea and the sand.

She sighed with pleasure.

Dean helped her out of the taxi, and while he went to get their bags and pay the driver, Jodie looked up at the building. Balconies jutted out, all facing the water. There would be a fantastic view from each one. The scent of lavish blooms wafted all around her, and she took several deep breaths for the pleasure of soaking up the aromas.

"Ready?"

Jodie turned and saw Dean waiting by the door, their bags in hand. "Sorry," she said. "I'm awestruck." She walked over to the door, opened it for him and then followed him across a large lobby to the elevators.

She pushed the button and the doors silently opened. Once inside, she asked, "Which floor?"

"The top one." She nodded and pushed the fourth-floor button.

When the doors opened, Jodie discovered there was only one set of double doors on the floor. Dean put their bags down, reached into his pocket for a key and opened one of the doors.

He stepped back for the bags and nodded. "After you, Ms. Cameron."

She hurried inside only to come to an abrupt stop, causing him to drop the bags just inside the door. "Oh, Dean, I've never seen anything like this. It looks like the set of a Hollywood movie about the rich and famous."

He closed the door and followed her into the room. "Pretty impressive, I'll admit. Would you like a tour?"

The condo encircled the elevator shaft, with windows looking out in all directions. She saw the well-stocked kitchen, the formal dining room with a mahogany table that could easily seat twelve people and three spacious bedrooms, each with its own bathroom and balcony. She thought the word for them in Hawaii was *lanai* but wasn't certain.

"Pick whichever bedroom you like," Dean said after their tour.

"Which one would you like?" she asked, feeling overwhelmed with choices.

"Doesn't matter."

"Mmm." She paused in the doorway of one. The room seemed the size of a basketball court. The view drew her to the window. "This will be fine," she murmured, opening the door to the outside.

She could hear the sound of the waves rolling onto the beach, the rhythm soothing to her ear. When she turned around, Dean was no longer there. He'd placed her bag on the bed.

Jodie wandered into the bathroom, which was larger

than her living room in Chicago. She smiled. She could quickly become used to living like this. All she could think was, Wow.

Suddenly feeling energized despite the long trip, she quickly unpacked, changed into a pair of cotton slacks and a sleeveless blouse and went back to the main room.

Dean was at the bar, pouring himself a drink. "Want one?" he asked as she walked in.

"Water will be fine. I'm not much of a drinker. I thought I'd go down and wander on the beach for a while."

"Aren't you hungry? I thought we could go eat first."

She thought about it. "Yes, as a matter of fact, I am. I suppose there will be plenty of daylight after we finish eating."

The restaurant was next to the complex. One side was open with tables and chairs inside and out. Jodie noticed there were only a few people at the tables. She glanced at her watch. "I suppose it's a little early to be eating according to local time."

"Doesn't matter. They're used to customers coming in at all hours. They're open twenty-four hours a day."

Once seated, Jodie picked up her menu and started reading the items listed. She yawned and hastily covered her mouth.

Dean watched her for a moment in silence before speaking. "You're going to want to go to sleep early tonight despite your nap on the plane, but if you can manage to stay awake, you'll adjust to the time change quicker."

"The steady sounds of the surf are so soothing. I hope I don't fall asleep with my nose in the salad."

Dean picked up his water glass and held it out. "Here's to our working vacation together."

Jodie picked up her glass and lightly tapped it against his. "I appreciate the invitation." She yawned again. "The way I'm feeling now, I could sleep the entire week away."

Once their food arrived, there was no more conversation. Jodie didn't want to chatter; that wasn't her style. Since they'd already commented on the beauty surrounding them, she could think of nothing to say to him.

By the time they finished eating, the sun was low in the west. Dean walked beside her in silence, his hands in his pockets, as she made her way to the sandy beach.

As the sky darkened, they watched the lights appear along the shoreline before turning back toward the condo. Walking in the sand would be an adjustment, but if she walked like this every day, she'd be in great shape when she returned home.

She smiled at the thought.

"What do you find so amusing?" he asked, stopping as she did to empty the sand from her shoes. He followed her example.

"I was thinking what a workout walking in the sand is. If I'm not in shape now, I will be by the time we leave."

"Probably."

A man of few words. Not that she cared. Tomorrow she would be up with the sun and she intended to enjoy every minute she was here.

After Jodie went to her room, Dean took a shower, dried off and stretched out on the bed.

He thought about Rachel. His anger at the abrupt way she'd dismissed him had caught him off guard. He'd learned many years ago to keep his emotions locked down.

He considered himself to be a thinking man who wasn't swayed by irrational feelings. But when Rachel had blown up at him—*inconsiderate* and *unfeeling* were the nicest things she'd called him—he'd felt an anger he hadn't experienced in a long time.

She hadn't given him a chance to explain. And she'd made it clear she wanted nothing more to do with him.

He had no problem with that and he was thankful he hadn't told her about his plans. Jodie had been right. He'd needed to get away for a few days. Seeing her excitement and enthusiasm this evening had caused him to look at everything through her eyes.

He couldn't remember a time when he'd been that joyous about anything.

Yes, having Jodie here with him might teach him how to enjoy life a little better.

He bet she'd been protected from the harsher realities of life until her—what? boyfriend? fiancé? she hadn't said—pulled his stupid stunt.

He smiled at the way she'd handled the situation. She'd faced the clod and gotten rid of him. But she'd suffered. Why else would she now be too busy to date much?

He turned and adjusted his pillow, willing himself to sleep. Instead his thoughts circled around Jodie. She'd looked so different today when she'd arrived at the airport, wearing formfitting jeans, a sweater, ankle boots and a parka.

The cold had turned her cheeks and nose a rosy hue, and he couldn't help wondering why he'd only noticed today how attractive she was. She was more than attractive, actually. *Beautiful* was an overused word and it didn't quite fit her, but it came close. He liked her looks. He liked and had always appreciated her frankness and her refusal to be intimidated by him. Jodie worked hard and earned every penny of her salary. She was smart and he valued her judgment.

He'd be lost without her.

At least she'd still be with the company. He hoped she could find someone as efficient to replace her.

He wanted this trip to be special for her. He'd get in touch with Furukawa tomorrow to set up a meeting. Once they met, he'd know if he had a chance of setting up some security systems for him.

He settled into sleep, planning the next day's activities.

"So much for plans," he muttered to himself the next morning when he discovered Jodie wasn't still in bed. He'd ordered breakfast from the restaurant, and when it had arrived, he'd knocked on her door.

When she hadn't answered, he'd eased the door open and discovered her room to be empty.

He sat at the kitchen bar, sipped his coffee and ate some of the delicious fruit that seemed to come with each meal. He'd arranged to have several newspapers brought to him each morning, so he read them while he absently ate.

Eventually Dean wandered over to the window and looked down at the beach.

The water looked peaceful this morning and there were several people on the beach, some walking and some relaxed in recliners, reading.

He watched as a lithe young woman came out of the water and grabbed her towel. He watched her for a few minutes before he recognized Jodie.

Her blond hair clung to her head in a beguiling helmet. Her face glowed with pleasure as she quickly dried off and placed her towel on the sand.

Dean couldn't take his eyes off her. Why had he never noticed her trim waist and curvaceous backside. In a one-piece bright red swimsuit cut high on the thighs, she could have posed for the cover of *Sports Illustrated* magazine.

She slicked her hands over her hair before ruffling it with her fingers. She had a way of moving that was quite sensuous. Why had he never noticed?

Dean realized that he wasn't the only male taking notice of her. As he watched, one of the men walked over and spoke to her. Dean turned away. It was none of his business what she did or who she met. So why was he bothered by seeing another man come on to her? There was absolutely no reason for him to feel so possessive about his secretary. She was free to enjoy her vacation in whatever manner she wanted.

He looked back down at them. The male said something to her and she laughed and turned away.

She laughed.

She didn't laugh around him.

With fresh resolve, he turned back to the papers on the counter and scanned them. He looked at his watch. He felt restless and unsettled, and it was too early to call his prospective client. He wondered how things were going at the office. His second in command could handle anything that came up. He knew the business as well as Dean did.

Dean paced to the window and looked at the sea, the mountains and finally the beach. She was alone now, but that didn't seem to bother the men who noticed her. He hoped they got their eyeful.

Dean turned away. He could go down there, maybe do a little swimming...except he hadn't packed a suit. Well, he could walk along the beach, but then the sand would fill his shoes.

The clothes he'd chosen to bring weren't suitable here. Of course, he'd be working, so it probably wouldn't matter. But if he wasn't working, what then? He shook his head in frustration. What did people do on vacation? After a moment he picked up the phone and called the office.

The sun was high overhead by the time Jodie gathered up her towels and beach bag to go search for something to eat. She'd go shower and change clothes and wander down the beach. There was bound to be a place other than the restaurant that was nearby.

She'd had great fun this morning and had met several people who, like her, were there enjoying the warm weather and beautiful scenery with no regrets about missing winter on the mainland.

She'd met a couple on their honeymoon, another celebrating their thirtieth wedding anniversary and a young couple with two little girls playing in the shallows.

Two or three guys had stopped and introduced themselves. One of them said he was on the beach each morning and would probably see her again. Another told her that today was his last day there and he intended to enjoy the water to the very last minute.

When she let herself into the condo, Jodie knew Dean

wasn't there. She wasn't certain how he managed to do it, but his charged energy filled whatever space surrounded him. When he wasn't there, the place was peaceful.

She looked around and saw a pile of newspapers beside a chair and the remains of breakfast on the kitchen counter. He'd ordered for both of them, she discovered, lifting a lid. She ate a brioche and then grabbed a banana. Delicious. That should tide her over while she showered and dressed.

Peering into the mirror after her shower, Jodie touched her nose. Yes, she'd definitely gotten some sun. She was going to have to be very careful not to burn.

She rubbed more sunscreen into her skin before she went into her bedroom to dress.

Jodie had splurged on her new clothes, telling herself that a vacation in Hawaii deserved tropical wear. She chose a pair of sandals, walking shorts and a sleeveless blouse that matched her blue eyes.

She left the condo and waited for the elevator. When the doors opened, Dean stood there. He was the first to speak.

"Going down?" he intoned politely.

She laughed. "Yes, please," she said, stepping into the elevator.

"I came up to see if you were here and wanted to get something to eat."

"You read my mind. I thought I'd walk along the beach and get something from one of the little restaurants I saw earlier."

He put his hands in his pockets. "I take it you enjoyed your morning?"

"Very much. How was yours?"

"I talked to Furukawa this morning. He said he could see me day after tomorrow, so I guess I'll be hanging around here for the next couple of days." He glanced at her and then away. "I think I'm going to need some pointers on how to take a vacation. I hope you're up for the job."

Jodie smiled at him. "Oh, I'm sure you'll get the hang of it soon."

The doors opened and they stepped into the lobby.

"I've called the office twice in hopes of learning about some crisis that only I could handle," he said with a slight smile. "Unfortunately everything is running smoothly."

He sounded so disgruntled that Jodie laughed. "It's not that bad, I'm sure."

"I asked around to find out what people usually do here besides visit the beach." He reached into his shirt pocket. "I found there are all sorts of things to see, if you'd be interested."

They walked out toward the water and walked along the edge.

He offered her the brochures and she eagerly took them. She looked over the various places of interest.

"There's so much to do and see."

By mutual agreement they turned toward a small café that caught their attention. Once seated, they glanced over the menu. Jodie ordered a large salad and Dean had a sandwich.

She continued to look through the brochures. "I'm amazed. We could spend a month and probably not see everything." She pointed to one of the brochures. "We can attend a luau," she said hopefully. "Or have you already been to one?"

"'Fraid not. I wasn't here long enough to do any sightseeing. I'm game for whatever appeals to you."

"Mmm," she said thoughtfully, thumbing through the brochures. "We could explore the other islands, charter a helicopter to look around at everything, check out the mountains or turn into slugs and lie on the beach all week."

He couldn't seem to take his eyes off her. She glowed with enthusiasm, something he'd rarely felt. "Sounds like a plan." He glanced at his watch and reached for his cell phone. "I'll make reservations for the luau and then I thought I might rent a car so I can do some shopping."

Her brows lifted. "You want to go to a mall? Dean, you have hidden depths!"

"I'm embarrassed to say that I didn't really pack the right clothes." He glanced down toward his feet. "I'm going to need to go native and get some sandals, maybe a couple pair of shorts, as well. And no self-respecting tourist could leave the islands without owning an authentic Hawaiian shirt."

She laughed. "Good for you. Step number one—dress for the occasion. Do you want me to go with you?"

He froze. Of course he wanted her with him. He realized that he'd presumed she'd go.

He cleared his throat. "Unless there's something else you'd like to do."

"I love to shop. Stick with me, kid, and I'll show you a pro at work."

He touched her hand. "Thank you."

She grinned at him. "You may not feel so grateful after I drag you through a few stores."

"I'll take my chances."

As a general rule, Dean disliked shopping, but then he'd never before gone on a spree with Jodie Cameron. They wandered through one of the malls and listened while groups of the locals played ukuleles and serenaded the shoppers.

"I used to play one of those when I was a kid," she confided as they stood and listened.

"Were you any good?"

"Well, I won't go so far as to say that, but I learned three or four basic chords that worked for most songs. What I lacked in talent I made up for in enthusiasm." She looked up at him and laughed, wrinkling her nose.

She was adorable.

"You'll have to play for me sometime," he said.

"Oooh, nooo, I don't think so. I haven't touched one in years. I don't know what happened to the one I had."

"Then we'll add that to our shopping list. One ukulele for you to serenade me with each evening. There are all kinds of working vacations. Who knows? You may launch a new career."

"You have no idea what you're asking," she replied ominously before she ruined the effect with a chuckle.

Dean followed Jodie in and out of various stores, in awe of her shopping talents. She knew immediately whether something would work for him and wasted no time looking at the rest.

She finally sent him back to a dressing room to try on several of the items she'd chosen. While she waited, Jodie wandered over to the gift-shop section of the store. She cheerfully bought gifts for everyone in the family as well as several of her friends.

She'd just paid for them when she saw Dean come out wearing a pair of shorts that fit him like a glove and a short-sleeved shirt with a tropical print.

"Wow. You look gorgeous," she said without thinking. When he turned an interesting shade of red, she realized what she'd said. "Oh! I'm sorry. I shouldn't have—"

"Oh, no. Don't apologize. You've just made my day. I don't believe anyone has every applied that word to me."

"Turn around," she said, still feeling a little awkward.

She checked the fit of the shirt across his shoulders and tried to ignore the way the shorts curved over his muscular butt. "You'll do," she said in a croak. Jodie cleared her throat. "What about the others? Did you like them?"

"Yeah. I'm getting all three shorts and a few extra shirts." He glanced down at his bare feet. "I, uh, didn't think my black socks and shoes went with the outfit."

"Good thinking. It just so happens the shoe department is right over there. Let's see what size you are and we'll get you fixed up right away."

By the time they reached the condo it was late afternoon and both of them had their arms full of packages. Once inside, they dumped them in the middle of the floor.

"I think we bought out the stores," he said, staring at the pile in wonderment.

"I still can't believe you actually bought a ukulele. You must be a glutton for punishment."

"How can you be in Hawaii and not want to play some of their songs? Now you have the songbook to help you."

"Uh-huh," Jodie replied, sounding skeptical. She looked around. "All right. Let's sort them out."

"What did you sneak off and buy while I was trying on shoes?" Dean asked, sorting through and picking out his purchases.

"A dress to wear for the luau tonight. I thought as long as you're going native, I might as well join you."

They carried the packages and sacks to their respective bedrooms. Before going into hers, Jodie looked at him and said, "I'm going to need a nap if I'm going to stay up late tonight."

"I was thinking along the same lines. I'll set my alarm to ring in a couple of hours."

"Thanks."

Once inside her room, Jodie leaned against the closed door, dropping her packages. What in the world was wrong with her! She felt as though scales had dropped from her eyes. How could she ever have thought Dean wasn't attractive? Maybe it was the environment and seeing him away from the business. He seemed so earnest about learning how to vacation. She wondered if he'd ever done anything like this before. How sad if he hadn't.

What bothered her was the amused affection she'd felt for him all afternoon as they'd looked at clothes. When she'd run her hands across his shoulders, she'd felt the ripple of muscle beneath her fingers and had a sudden longing to continue touching him.

Without a doubt, she was in trouble. They'd been gone two days, and here she was getting all tingly whenever she looked at him.

Of course, she wasn't going to do anything about it. That

would be too foolish to consider. But there was no law against looking—if she could keep herself from doing something obvious, like drooling.

Five

His wristwatch alarm woke Dean and he was surprised how soundly he'd slept. He sat on the side of the bed and looked out the sliding glass doors. The sky was turning to a deep blue as the day faded. Checking his watch again, he went down the hallway and knocked on Jodie's door.

There was no response.

Finally he opened the door and saw her sound asleep, a cover thrown over her.

"Jodie?"

No answer.

He walked over to the bed. "Jodie, it's time to wake up."

"'Kay," she mumbled into the pillow without moving.

Giving in to temptation, he turned on the radio on her night table and turned up the volume, which certainly did the trick. She jerked up on all fours and looked all around in alarm.

"Sorry. Didn't mean to startle you," he said, trying not to smile.

She sat back on her heels. "Oh. Guess I should have warned you. I'm a sound sleeper."

"I gathered that. I'll let you get ready and meet you in the living room."

"Are you going to wear your new clothes?"

"Absolutely," he said and removed himself from the room.

"Wow," she said to him when she joined him later. "You've definitely gone native."

"When in Rome…" he said with a shrug, trying not to stare.

She wore a tropical print with a sea-blue background. It looked to be wrapped around her, revealing her shapely shoulders and hugging her delectable body. There was little evidence of the secretary tonight.

"What do you think?" she asked and slowly turned in a circle.

He swallowed. "Looks good. Fits nicely."

She laughed. "Actually it's a wrap. The clerk showed me how to put it on. I'm wearing an honest-to-goodness sarong."

That's when he knew he was in serious trouble.

She walked toward him. "I also bought this shell necklace to go with it." She took his arm. "This is going to be so much fun, I just know it."

He silently agreed—if he could survive the evening without grabbing her and kissing her senseless.

* * *

Jodie decided that the luau was everything she'd dreamed about and more. Foods—some she liked better than others—and mai tais, a drink she'd never had before and found delicious, all added to the occasion. The native dances called to her. She had no idea how the women moved their hips so rapidly to the beat of the drums.

It was the drums that kept her pulse throbbing. She glanced at Dean beside her, who seemed to be enjoying himself and the entertainment. She glanced back at the young women. They really were something. Every man there watched them with avid eyes.

She leaned against his shoulder and gave him a slight nudge. "Think you could dance and play the drums like that?"

He glanced at her. "I wouldn't attempt to try. Are you enjoying yourself?"

"Oh, yes."

"You might want to go easy on the rum drinks. They have a delayed kick."

She looked at her almost-empty glass. Was that her second one or her third? "Oh. They taste like fruit juice." She glanced over at his glass. "What are you drinking?"

"Piña colada. Want to try it?"

"No, thanks." She sipped on her drink. "There can't be much rum in this or I'd be able to taste it."

"You're not much of a drinker, are you?"

"Not really." She grinned. "But I'm on vacation, so I thought I'd indulge."

The drums came to a sudden stop and Jodie looked around. The dancing girls were carrying leis in their arms and placing them around each guest's neck.

She liked the way Dean looked with the flowers draped over his shoulders.

"Are you ready to go back to the condo?" he asked.

"Sure." They had walked along the beach to this location and would walk back. He helped her up and she realized that she was a little dizzy. Maybe Dean had been right about the drinks.

He slipped his arm around her waist and she naturally did the same to him. He looked good tonight. The shorts he'd chosen to wear showed off his muscular legs. She smoothed his shirt beneath her hand, enjoying the feel of him. She smiled to herself. This was definitely a romantic evening, and Dean was fulfilling her fantasy of a midnight stroll with someone she cared about.

As they ambled along the edge of the water, she looked up into the sky and said, "I've never seen the stars so bright."

"Big cities tend to put off too much light to see the stars."

"That explains it." She rested her head on his shoulder. The sound of the surf added a sensuous rhythm to the night. She'd never been this close to Dean before and she inhaled the scent of his aftershave.

His warmth radiated along her side, and her body tingled everywhere they touched.

"It's going to be hard to top this experience," she said dreamily to break the silence that had fallen between them. They turned toward the path that led to the condos. When he didn't answer, she lifted her head and looked at him. He looked grim as he stared ahead of them. She eased away from him and promptly stumbled.

He grabbed her arm to keep her from falling.

"I think you were right about the drinks," she said ruefully. "I'm beginning to feel the effects."

He opened the door to the lobby for her and waited until they were in the elevator alone before he said, "I'm afraid you're going to have a bad headache in the morning."

They stepped out of the elevator and he unlocked the door to the condo. Once inside, she replied, "Probably. But it will be worth it."

He nodded. "Hope you feel the same way in the morning." They walked toward their bedrooms. They reached hers first.

"Thank you for tonight. I hope you weren't bored," she said.

"Not at all. I don't think I gave the business a thought for, oh, at least thirty minutes." He grinned at her.

She smiled. "I don't know what I'm going to do about you."

"A good-night kiss would be nice."

His comment caught her off guard. It was the last thing she'd expected to hear from him.

"Of course," she said and leaned toward him. She closed her eyes, expecting a peck on her cheek. Instead he slowly drew her into his arms and brushed his lips against hers. What was happening to her? Was it the rum that suddenly made her melt against him...and put her arms around his neck?

By the time he loosened his grip, they were both gasping for air.

"I've wanted to do that all evening," he said hoarsely.

"I didn't know," she murmured and rubbed her finger

along his strong jawline and cheek. Jodie attempted a smile. "Well, good night," she managed to say before she stepped into her room and closed the door.

Dean closed his eyes and stood there. What had he done? Was he out of his mind? He'd taken advantage of the fact that she was there with him, which was unconscionable.

And why hadn't she slapped his face!

Now he knew exactly how she felt pressed against him, how she tasted as her soft mouth opened to his like a budding flower. He'd not forget it, nor would he forget the fact that they still had five days together before heading back to Chicago.

He shook his head and strode into his bedroom. He stripped off his clothes and headed for a much-needed shower and some stern self-talk. Getting involved with Jodie Cameron would be the height of recklessness.

Unfortunately for his peace of mind, he'd discovered tonight that he'd been involved with her for years.

The first thing Jodie knew the next morning when she opened her eyes was that Dean had grossly underestimated the effect of the mai tais. She didn't have just a headache; concrete drills were going off inside her head.

The second thing that registered was the heavenly scent of freshly brewed coffee wafting its way into her room. The thought of coffee was the call of the sirens that drew her out of bed. She put on the thick terry-cloth robe that was in the bathroom, carefully brushed her hair—even her scalp hurt this morning—and went in search of the elixir that might help her live.

Dean sat at the kitchen bar, next to the coffeepot, reading the paper. He glanced up when she moved carefully toward him.

"How're you feeling?" he asked, his voice low.

She almost whimpered. Even that much noise made her head hurt worse. "I should have stopped after the first drink," she whispered. She filled the large coffee mug sitting beside the pot to the brim and immediately lifted it to her mouth. It was too hot to drink, but she could live off the aroma for a moment.

"Aspirin will help," he said, nodding toward a bottle there on the counter.

She filled a glass with water, took a couple of tablets and sat down on the bar stool next to Dean.

He wore shorts, a shirt and sandals. He looked rested and fit. She could almost hate a person for that when she felt like something that had washed up on the shore. He continued to read the paper, and for the first time she fully appreciated his taciturn personality.

She sipped her coffee and squinted out the window. The sun had been up for hours, but at this particular moment she didn't care if she ever saw the sun again.

Dean laid the paper on the counter and got up. He walked over to the expanse of windows and drew the drapes closed.

"How did you know?" she asked with relief when he seated himself once again. He flicked on the small light near where he sat.

"I've overindulged myself a few times in my thirty-odd years. I know what it's like."

She placed her mug on the counter and rested her head in her hands. "The drinks tasted so innocent. I had no idea…" Her voice faded.

He raised his hand to rub her back in sympathy but thought better of it. He cleared his throat. "I know the idea doesn't sound appealing, but you'll feel better once you get some food inside you."

"You are absolutely right. The idea doesn't sound at all appealing."

He grinned and picked up the phone. After ordering them both breakfasts, he hung up and looked at her. "Nibble on some toast, drink some juice—"

"Are you kidding?" she asked in horror, dropping her hands from her head. "I'll probably never drink another glass of juice again."

"It wasn't the fruit juice that caused your pain."

She groaned. "You're always so logical."

"So are you, most of the time. You'll feel better as the day wears on."

"That's a relief. Right now I'd have to get better to die."

He chuckled but didn't say anything else.

When their meal arrived, he opened the door and took the tray, giving the waiter a tip before closing the door and bringing the food to the bar.

Jodie eyed the tray skeptically at the same time her stomach growled. Like it or not, she needed to eat something.

Did Dean always have to be right?

Miraculously by midafternoon she was beginning to feel almost human again. Not well enough to go outside just yet, but better. Anything was an improvement.

Dean had left after breakfast and hadn't yet returned. She wondered where he'd gone. Not that it was any of her business. He might have hooked up with one of the women they'd met at the luau last night.

She frowned at the thought.

What was the matter with her? He'd dated a number of women since she'd worked for him and she hadn't given the matter a thought. Until last night, she hadn't figured he had much passion in him.

She'd definitely been proved wrong there. She groaned at the memory of her response to him. If she hadn't felt so awful this morning, she probably couldn't have faced him.

At least he'd been a gentleman and hadn't mentioned what had happened last night.

Jodie finally went in and showered, the water having its usual soothing effect on her. By the time she dressed and returned to the living room, she felt human again.

She heard the key in the door and glanced around as Dean let himself inside. When he saw her, he grinned and said, "Ignore the ransom note, I managed to escape."

Six

Jodie jumped up and stared at him in shock. "You were kidnapped?" she asked, her voice going up.

He paused before closing the door. "Sorry, I was just making a joke. I was gone longer than I expected to be." She lowered herself back into the chair, feeling silly for overreacting. "How are you feeling?" he asked, making himself comfortable on the nearby sofa.

"Much better than this morning, thank you."

"Did you eat anything for lunch?"

"I ordered some soup. I wasn't up to going downstairs."

"I've set up sightseeing tours for the rest of our stay here. We'll meet Steve Furukawa for lunch tomorrow in Honolulu. While we're there, we'll see the Pearl Harbor Memorial and whatever else looks interesting. There are some great places to see while we're here. I think you'll feel well enough tomorrow to enjoy them."

"Oh. Well. That's nice. I mean, I'm looking forward to it."

"Do you think you're up to sitting out on the beach for a while? The fresh air will do you good."

She nodded. "Good idea. I'll go change."

He got up when she did. "I'll do the same."

As she changed into a two-piece suit she'd bought the day before, Jodie realized that she hadn't seen Dean in his swimsuit. He'd reported that it fit, and that was all that had mattered to her.

She just wished she wasn't so physically aware of him.

They rode the elevator in silence. Jodie wore the matching cover-up to the suit. Dean had on one of his shirts but hadn't bothered to button it. They both had large towels with them.

She did her best not to stare at his chest. Instead she trained her eyes on his face, only to discover that he was looking at her with a great deal of interest.

"New suit?" he asked as they left the building.

"Yes." She stopped and put on her dark sunglasses.

Once on the beach, Jodie carefully laid out one of her towels and slipped off the beach cover.

"Very nice," he said and she glanced around. He stood with his hands resting on his hips, obviously waiting for her to finish making her beach nest.

Dean stripped to his swimsuit was a Dean she'd never known existed. It unnerved her to have all her ideas about who the man was turned upside down. When did he have time to work out, which he had to do to be in such good shape?

She sat and he tossed his towel down and sat beside her.

She wished that she could forget the kiss they'd shared. It had been an aberration; certainly not the norm. However, every time she looked at his mouth, she remembered how his lips had felt touching hers.

The man certainly knew how to kiss!

"This is nice," he said several minutes later. "Is the air helping your head?"

"You're being nice to me," she finally replied. "And it's making me nervous."

"Why? Aren't I always nice to you?"

"Shall I be polite or honest?"

"You're talking about the office, aren't you?"

"That's the person I know—or thought I knew."

He leaned back on his elbows. "Well, we've moved past that, haven't we? After last night?"

She groaned. "I was hoping you'd forgotten about that."

He turned onto his side, propping himself up on an elbow. "Why? We'd had fun at the party and we ended the evening the way most dates are ended—with a kiss."

She slipped her shades down her nose and looked at him. "This is not a dating situation, Dean. I happened to be available to come here because my boss gave me the time off."

"Worked out well, didn't it?" He grinned. "You've opened my eyes regarding several things about my life. I'm hoping you can continue to teach me how to relax and enjoy myself. You've done a good job so far."

Jodie sat up and folded her legs into a yoga position. "What's going on, anyway? What do you hope to accomplish while we're here, other than gaining another client?"

"I want to get to know you better. I've already told you."

"Why? You've known me for years and have never looked at me the way you have since we arrived here."

He chuckled, and despite her practical nature, she was charmed by the sound. A week ago she would have sworn he didn't know how.

"I've never seen you in a swimsuit before...or a sarong, for that matter," he offered casually. Then his tone changed. "I find you fascinating. You have so many facets to your personality, and I've discovered that I want to learn each and every one of them."

"Dean. We'll be back at the office next week and none of this will have mattered. I don't want to make anything more out of our time together than it is."

"I guess that means we won't be sleeping together."

Chuck was right. All men thought about was getting an available woman in bed with them! Then she realized he was laughing at her reaction.

"You're teasing, right?"

"Actually I'm enjoying the expressions running across your face. Just so we're clear, I wouldn't say no if you decide to take me up on my offer."

She shook her head and stretched out on her towel once more. Her heart raced so fast she was certain he could see it pounding in her chest. She knew he was teasing.

He had to be teasing, hoping to fluster her.

Well, she was made of sterner stuff.

Her tone casual, Jodie said, "I'll think about it."

He gave a whoop of laughter and said, "You do that," and then trotted to the water's edge to wade out into the water.

She watched him dive into a wave and appear on the other side. Of course she wasn't going to sleep with him.

That would be the dumbest thing possible for her to do. Okay, so he wouldn't turn her down. So what? To him it would be a casual fling. But becoming intimate with him would change her life. Long after he'd forgotten about this trip, memories would haunt her. It would be impossible to work closely with him without recalling what they had shared.

No. The answer was no.

Jodie stood and walked toward the water.

The water felt good to her, cooling her overheated body. Jodie lowered herself into the water and began a leisurely crawl, feeling her muscles work as she glided through the water.

When Dean spotted her, he angled toward her, cleaving the water in strong strokes.

She smiled at him as he drew near. "I decided to see if the water felt as good as it looks…and it does."

"How's your head?"

"Still on my shoulders. From now on, I'll have one drink and stop, no matter how good it tastes to me."

They continued to swim parallel to the beach, Dean keeping pace with her. Eventually they waded toward the shore together and continued walking until they reached their towels. He quickly dried off and waited for her to gather her things.

"What would you like to do this evening?"

There was a provocative question if she'd ever heard one. "You don't have to entertain me while we're here, you know."

"True, but we've both got to eat and I'd prefer not to eat alone."

"That makes sense, I guess," she replied. "Do you have someplace in mind?"

"Actually I do. I ate there the last time I was here and the Polynesian food is well prepared. If you've never tried it, you're in for a treat."

They stepped inside the elevator.

Finally she nodded. "All right. Thank you for suggesting it."

That evening Jodie looked around the softly lit room, the hurricane lamps on each table making an oasis of light. "You're right," she said to Dean, "this is a great place with a distinct atmosphere."

"I'm glad you're enjoying it. Do you like the food I ordered?"

"It's different but really good. Thanks for bringing me." She sipped her iced tea. "How should I behave toward your prospective client tomorrow?"

He studied her for a moment in silence. Finally he said, "No striptease, no hula and no playing the ukulele."

"Striptease? I've never done anything like that in my—" She stopped. "You're teasing me again."

"Can't resist. You're so much fun to watch when you react."

"Fine. Just for that, I'll take my ukulele and sing all through lunch."

"You can sing?"

"No."

"A threat then."

"Very much a threat."

"You'll do fine tomorrow. You know our business very well. Speaking of which, once we get back, I'm going to talk to Frank Godfrey about putting you into his department as soon as possible rather than waiting until you graduate. We're only talking about a few months. So treat tomorrow like a training session as I present what we have to offer and answer Furukawa's questions."

"You're going to promote me now?"

"Not this minute, no. But when we get back to the office I'll start the ball rolling."

"That's wonderful news! Thank you so much."

"Don't thank me. Frank's a good supervisor and he'll work you hard learning how we go about providing the necessary equipment to keep our clients secure."

Over dessert and coffee Jodie asked, "Why are you promoting me now?"

"What do you mean?"

"Well, you don't have a secretary lined up to replace me, for one thing."

He groaned. "Don't remind me. But that shouldn't take too long."

"Well, um…"

"Why do you make such a point that I'm difficult to work for?"

"Because you are difficult to work for. Or have you forgotten how many secretaries walked out on you before I was hired?"

He pulled his earlobe and looked uncomfortable. "I've mellowed since then."

"I'll take your word for it."

"Haven't I?"

"You've mellowed because I learned how you like to work."

"That doesn't sound too hard."

"That's true. It doesn't." She looked around. "Shall we go?"

"Wait a minute. I'm missing something here, Jodie. Tell me."

"You want your office to run smoothly. I know your likes and dislikes enough to anticipate how and what you want, that's all."

"In other words, you can read my mind."

"Not at all."

"That's good to know considering some of my thoughts while on this trip."

A burst of heat engulfed her and she knew she'd turned a fiery red. Jodie picked up her water glass and drank. When she had emptied the glass, she studied it without looking up.

"I'm sorry. I didn't mean to embarrass you."

Why should he apologize when she certainly wouldn't want him to learn of any of her thoughts these past few days?

"It's all right."

He brushed his fingers across the back of her hand. "No, it isn't. I've made you uncomfortable around me and that's the last thing I want. You're right. It's time to go."

They drove back to the condo listening to music. Once inside the condo, Jodie said, "If you'll excuse me, I think I'll go to bed."

"Of course. Sleep well."

Dean watched her walk out of the room, still irritated with himself. What was the matter with him, coming on to her like this? He'd been off balance where she was concerned since he'd first seen her at the airport.

He wandered over to the window and looked out. The view continued to be spectacular, even at night. While he stood there, he thought about their trip to Oahu the next day.

In an airplane.

In a small airplane.

Of course, Jodie knew they would have to fly. From what he remembered, the flight was a short one. They barely got into the air before it was time to land. The small plane could make the experience a little bumpy since the pilot flew at a reasonably low altitude.

Perhaps the flight here from Chicago had helped to allay her fears about flying. He could only hope.

One look at her face the next morning and he knew his hope had been futile. Not that she said anything. However, despite the slight tan she'd gotten thus far on the trip, she was a pasty white. Not a good sign.

Without a word, he poured her a cup of coffee. He'd been up since dawn and had already had several cups.

"Thank you," she murmured, immediately picking up the cup and sipping.

He waited until she set the cup down and then casually asked, "How are you this morning?"

"Okay," she said quietly.

"I believe our flight leaves in a couple of hours."

She didn't comment.

"Jodie?"

Startled, she looked at him. "Yes?"

"Are you nervous about the flight?"

"How did you know?"

"I remembered you were a little nervous—" there was an understatement if he'd ever made one "—on our flights here."

She nodded. "I don't mind it once we get in the air and level out. It's the taking off and landing that bothers me."

"Unfortunately that's what we'll be doing this morning."

"Oh. Well, of course."

"Why don't we go downstairs and get some breakfast. Are you up for that?"

"Okay."

She didn't sound at all certain.

While they ate, he chatted about the office and some projects he was working on, trying to keep her mind off her upcoming ordeal. She responded in monosyllables.

Finally he said, "I thought we might go to the Big Island tomorrow. It will mean another short flight, but I've been told the volcano is something to behold."

She went from pasty white to an interesting color of green.

"Of course, if you don't want to go…"

"That's fine. Really. Whatever you want to do is fine with me."

Sure it was.

Dean checked his watch. "We should head for the airport soon. Do you need to go back to the condo?"

She shook her head.

Today she looked like the secretary he'd known for years. She had her hair pinned up—he hadn't realized how much he liked to see it down until now—and wore a lightweight suit. She looked like a business professional despite her pallor. Unfortunately for his peace of mind, he had the vision of her in a swimsuit and wearing a sarong. He would never view his efficient secretary in the same way now that he'd gotten to know her better.

She must have been hurt badly by the jerk she'd thought would be her husband. How else could he explain to himself the subdued person he'd known for the past five years?

Seeing her literally letting her hair down and enjoying herself had been a revelation to him.

Once in the car, he tried to make conversation by asking her about various subjects. She answered in monosyllables until he gave up and turned on the radio.

By the time they were seated in the smallish plane, he knew that the situation required drastic action.

He'd been on flights like this before. The plane took off at a steep angle. Since she'd admitted she'd never been on one this small, she probably would be startled.

"Jodie?"

"Mmm?"

He took her hand. "Do you know what I'd like to do right now?"

She turned and looked at him hopefully. "Get off the plane?"

He laughed. "Um, no. What I'd like to do is kiss you senseless."

Well, that certainly took her mind off flying. She stared at him in astonishment. "Why?" she asked starkly.

"Well, for one thing, you have the most kissable mouth

of anyone I've ever known." He looked down at their clasped hands. With his other hand, he stroked the back of her hand with his finger. "And you fit into my arms as though you were made just for me."

He felt her hand tremble and she turned a charming shade of red, which nicely replaced her ashen color.

The plane started moving. He lifted her hand to his mouth and kissed her palm, his tongue lightly touching her. She stiffened when they took off. He wasn't certain whether it was the kiss or the flight. So he leaned toward her and kissed her on the mouth.

Her lips trembled, and he took his time caressing her mouth with his lips and tongue. Slowly she responded and he forgot his reason for starting this in the first place.

An amused feminine voice spoke near his shoulder. "I'm sorry to interrupt you, sir, but I'd like to offer the two of you something to drink, if you like. We'll only be in the air for another twenty minutes."

Jodie pulled away from him and stared at her. "We're in the air?"

"Yes, ma'am." The flight attendant grinned. "I can understand your distraction."

Jodie looked at Dean. "You did that on purpose!"

Dean told the attendant to bring them some orange juice before he looked at Jodie. "I suppose I did. I've never accidentally kissed anyone."

She glanced out the window and blanched.

"From now on you'll sit in the aisle seat," he said briskly. "We're doing fine."

She turned and looked at him. "You know what I mean! You deliberately distracted me."

Once again he lifted her hand and kissed her palm. "Did it work?"

"I know I'm being ridiculous about flying."

"You just need to do it more often so you can get used to it."

"That's your prescription, Dr. Logan?"

"Absolutely. And here in the islands is a perfect place to practice. We'll make certain to visit each and every one of them."

"Oh, joy," she muttered.

Their drinks arrived and he let go of her hand.

The landing was as abrupt as the takeoff. Jodie squeezed his hand so hard she must have been cutting off circulation. But he didn't mind. She was adorable when she was vulnerable.

Once on the ground, Jodie felt giddy with relief despite her embarrassment. When she had finally let go of Dean's hand, it still had the imprints of her fingers on it.

They took a cab to the address Dean had. Once they arrived, Jodie asked, "Is this his office?"

"No. This is a private club for local businessmen. He said to give his name at the door."

Jodie waited while Dean spoke to the man who met them at the front door. The man looked at a list he carried on a clipboard, found Dean's name and nodded. He escorted them to a double door that was ornately engraved.

When Jodie walked in, she looked around her. There was a large bar made of teak to the right of the entrance. A maître d' met them at the top of the steps.

"We're here to meet Mr. Furukawa," Dean said.

"Right this way, sir," the man replied.

The place was meticulously designed and elegantly decorated. The only sounds were the murmured voices of other diners, their voices muted by the thick carpeting underfoot. Pristine white tablecloths covered each table and they looked like islands floating on the deep red carpet.

The maître d' continued through the room until he reached an alcove that overlooked the water. Once they were seated, he poured ice water into glasses and said, "Your waiter will be with you shortly."

Once Jodie was certain he was out of earshot, she said, "The scent of money is everywhere."

Dean grinned. "I noticed."

She gazed at his mouth. Jodie discovered she had a little trouble breathing whenever he smiled at her. She couldn't forget the touch of his lips on hers.

"Sorry to keep you waiting," a newcomer said from behind her.

Dean stood and extended his hand. "Perfectly all right, Mr. Furukawa," he said.

"Please, call me Steve."

Steve wore a custom-made suit that showed off his trim figure and tanned face. His hair gleamed like polished pewter.

"Steve, I'd like you to meet Jodie Cameron, one of the employees with our firm."

Steve took her hand and bowed slightly. "It is a pleasure."

While they ordered and their meal was served, Jodie watched and listened as the men discussed several topics, none of which had anything to do with a possible security installation. She couldn't help but wonder why he'd brought her, unless the business meeting was to take place after their meal.

Dean included her in the conversation, and when Steve asked how she was enjoying Hawaii, she responded readily enough.

Once their plates were removed and they were left with fresh cups of coffee, Steve said, "I've been reading up on you, Dean."

"And?"

"You and your company have an excellent reputation in the security field. What kind of security do you offer?"

"We make certain that no unauthorized person can enter your place of business without a silent alarm going off, alerting the staff. We offer hidden surveillance cameras that record everyone who goes in or out. Security codes are installed and updated regularly. In addition, we install special software on each computer in your office that will also alert you should anyone attempt to gain illegal access to the company's computers."

"I see." Steve glanced at his watch. "I'd like you to see my setup and give me some idea of what your systems would cost to install and run."

Dean nodded. "Of course."

Steve signed for their meal and the three of them returned through the restaurant. Several people spoke to Steve while they made their way to the entrance.

By the time they reached the street, valet parking had his car waiting.

The men continued to chat during the drive. Jodie, in the backseat, made notes of the conversation that pertained to business, finally feeling as though she could be useful.

By the time they left Steve Furukawa that afternoon, he'd agreed to become one of the company's clients. On the way to the airport Dean called the office and left a voice-mail message for the legal department that he had a new client.

Once on the plane, Jodie—determined to ignore the butterflies in her stomach—said, "Your trip has been a success, hasn't it?"

Dean nodded. "Definitely. Thank you for taking such extensive notes. I'll fax them to the office so Lawrence Kendall will have the information he needs to prepare the contract." He studied her for a moment and then asked, "You doing okay?"

She nodded.

"Good. So shall we visit the volcano tomorrow?"

"I'd like that," she replied, hoping he didn't detect her lack of enthusiasm.

"Or we could stay at the condo and enjoy the beach area," he said casually.

"It's up to you."

"My only reason for suggesting the trip was to allow you to see more of the islands."

"Why don't we wait until the day before we leave then?"

"Whatever you say."

Once back at the condo, Dean said, "We have time to go for a swim before dark if you'd like."

"I'd like that." Jodie went into her room and closed the door. Somehow, some way, she would get through this week with the man she'd gotten to know here on the islands who only vaguely resembled her boss. The fact that she liked and enjoyed this new person unnerved her more than a little.

All she could hope was that once in the office again, he would assume his sardonic personality.

Seven

Saturday afternoon they left the condo for the last time and headed toward the airport.

They'd spent the earlier part of the day on the beach and swimming, chatting about their time there. Jodie hoped her manner hadn't betrayed how sad she was to be going home. Dean had made her laugh that morning. She so enjoyed his wry sense of humor.

She glanced at Dean driving the rental car. He'd already returned to his terse manner and stone face, which would help her adjust to the fact that the man she'd spent the week with was nothing like the man she worked with.

Once on the plane, Jodie picked up one of the magazines she'd bought and waited for takeoff.

Dean touched her hand and she looked at him. "Thank you for being here this week."

"I enjoyed it. I'm not looking forward to Chicago's winter, I can assure you."

She closed her eyes during takeoff and prayed that the pilot could get the large plane in the air without a problem since they were immediately over water.

Once they leveled off, the flight attendant brought their meals and drinks. After she ate, Jodie closed her eyes and willed herself to sleep, determinedly putting the islands and the memories there to the back of her mind.

They arrived in Chicago Sunday morning. Dean gathered their bags and said, "I'll take you home."

"Thank you."

"Wait here and I'll bring the car around."

While she waited, she looked out at the gray skies and the people huddled into their winter coats to get away from the wind. *Yes, Dorothy, you've returned to Kansas and Oz is only a memory.* There was nothing more tangible than the weather to remind her that her fantasy vacation had come to an end.

She saw a late-model sports car pull up to the curb, and Dean stepped out. She picked up her suitcase, and in a few strides he'd come inside and picked up the rest of their luggage. With customary efficiency Dean loaded the bags in the surprisingly roomy trunk and opened the passenger door for her.

Once they were both inside, he pulled away from the curb. "Where to?"

She gave him directions and settled into the comfortable seat. He drove with efficiency just as he did everything else. When he reached her apartment complex, she said, "You can let me out here. I can—"

"I'd like to see where you live," he said bluntly.

"Why?" she asked just as bluntly.

"No reason, really. Do you have a problem with my knowing where you live?"

"Of course not. Personnel has it on record."

"You've been really quiet this morning. Any particular reason?"

"I'm just tired. I had trouble sleeping on the plane."

"Well, now that you're home you can sleep the day away."

She directed him to the entrance of the underground parking and showed him her second parking space. He pulled in next to her red car.

"Yours?" he asked, getting out and going to the trunk.

"Yes."

He picked up her luggage, which included the ukulele case, locked his car with the remote and followed her to the elevator. Once inside, she pushed the button for her floor and they waited in silence.

When she opened her door and motioned for him to go ahead of her, he walked in. She'd hoped he would put the cases down in the hallway and leave. No such luck. He set them in the hallway and continued into the living room.

"Nice place," he said, glancing around.

"I like it."

He walked over to her and without a word took her in his arms and kissed her, taking his time. She didn't want to respond to him; she couldn't allow herself to respond to him and she was unnerved by how much she wanted to.

When he released her, his words were quietly prosaic. "I'll see you at work tomorrow," he said and let himself out.

Jodie stood there and stared at the door. With one kiss he had brought the fantasy home to Chicago. What was she going to do?

After she unpacked and began to wash clothes, she called Lynette. Kent answered.

"Hi, Aunt Jodie. Are you calling from Hawaii?"

"No, sweetheart. I'm back home. Is your mom there?"

"Uh-huh."

"May I speak to her?"

"Uh-huh."

She could still hear him breathing into the phone. She heard Lynette in the background say, "May I have the phone, please?"

Kent sounded fainter as he said, "Uh-huh."

Lynette took the phone and said, "Do you think I need to increase my son's vocabulary?"

Jodie replied, "Uh-huh."

They both laughed. "How was the trip? Did you throttle your boss? Toss him in the ocean? Drop him into one of the volcanoes? Tell me everything."

Her feelings toward Dean had changed so much in the week she'd been gone that for a moment she didn't understand why Lynette would say those things.

"Actually he was fun to be with. I enjoyed being there with him."

After a prolonged silence Lynette said, "Who is this? Hello? Was I cut off from my sister? Hello? Hello?"

Jodie chuckled. "Cut it out. And you needn't worry about my sanity. He was on vacation and I had an opportunity to see another side to him."

"Somehow I never expected to hear the words *fun* and *Dean Logan* in the same sentence coming from you. What in the world happened to turn Mr. Hyde into Dr. Jekyll?"

Jodie sighed. "Doesn't matter. Mr. Hyde was definitely present once we landed at the airport. By noon tomorrow I'll have forgotten completely the friendly, funny man I met on the island." The kiss didn't count.

"Speaking of meeting men, did you spot any good-looking hunks strolling the beaches?"

"Quite a few, actually," Jodie replied, grinning. "Of course, most of them were accompanied by professional swimsuit models. Or if they weren't, they should be."

"You can hold your own with the best of them, kiddo."

"I had at least ten pounds on the heaviest ones."

"And all in the right places. Did you have Dean drooling?"

Her throat tightened and for a moment she couldn't speak. Finally she said, "Not so you'd notice."

"Plan to come over tonight for dinner. I hope you took lots of photos so I can be envious and jealous and all that stuff."

Jodie laughed. "You are so full of it. You wouldn't be away that long from the kids."

"True. But I can dream. See you tonight."

Jodie turned off the handset and said, "Dreaming isn't real." She didn't need to tell Lynette that, of course. She needed to remind herself.

She took a nap before going over to Lynette and Chuck's. She carefully dressed and hoped that they couldn't read her face. Maybe they'd think the glow was all suntan. She could only hope.

Kent and Kyle greeted her at the door that evening with whoops and hollers that made her laugh.

"Boys!" Lynette said. "Hush or you'll wake Emily."

They immediately quieted. "Did you bring us something?" Kyle asked expectantly, eyeing the large shopping bag she carried.

"Kyle!" Lynette scolded. "You know better than that!" She hugged Jodie before she stepped back. "Don't you look great! The tan really emphasizes the color of your eyes."

Chuck joined them. "Looking good, little sis. Vacations obviously agree with you."

Jodie sat down on the sofa and immediately had two little boys eyeing the bag. She began to pull out various gifts, explaining where she'd found different ones. When she finished, she said to Lynette, "Dean bought me a ukulele."

"Did he know you play?"

"I made the mistake of telling him. Actually the chords came back to me fairly easily and I'm not too bad on the thing."

"Did you bring it with you?" Kent asked. "I didn't know you can play."

"No, I left it at the apartment. One of these days when you come to visit I'll get it out for you."

Eventually they sat down to eat. Everyone was full of questions and the time flew by. It was only when she got ready to leave that Lynette walked her to the door and quietly asked, "Something happened over there, didn't it?"

"What makes you think that?"

"Because I know you. There's a shadow in your eyes I've never seen before."

"I'm just tired. Traveling really wears me out."

"If you say so."

"It's probably the letdown of getting back home and picking up my routine again."

Lynette hugged her. "Okay. Then we'll see you Friday night, right?"

"Right."

Jodie let herself out of the warm house and into the cold. She hurried to her car and crawled inside. While she waited for the car to warm and the heater to kick on, Jodie thought about Lynette's comments.

Truly, nothing *had* happened except for a few shared kisses, and she had no intention of discussing her response to Dean with anyone. After all, the kisses had been an impulse of the moment...except for the one this morning. She hadn't needed the reminder that she was strongly attracted to Dean Logan, which wasn't very smart.

She turned on the car radio and listened to music during her drive home, determined to put him completely out of her mind.

Eight

"**W**ow! Look at you!" Betty said by way of greeting when Jodie walked into the office the next morning. "Quite a tan. You certainly stand out among all of us oatmeal-colored people. So where did you go?"

"Hawaii."

"Ooooh, well good for you. Does the boss know you took off the same week he did?"

"Yes. Is he in yet?"

"Haven't seen him, but that doesn't mean much. It's not unusual for him to get here before I do."

Jodie nodded and headed to her office.

Once there, she almost groaned at the sight of her desk covered in papers with notes attached, files stacked high and file drawers half-open. She glanced into his office and saw Dean at his desk, frowning at something he was reading.

She put her purse away and made coffee. While she waited for the coffee to brew, she sat and began to sort through the mess on her desk.

"Jodie? Is that you?"

She stood and walked over to his doorway. "Yes. How did you manage to go through so much work this morning?"

"Oh, that's from yesterday. I spent the day catching up on what's been happening. Is there coffee?"

She glanced over her shoulder. "Yes. I'll bring you some."

"Thanks," he said absently, leaning back in his chair, still reading.

There, you see? she told herself. He's already forgotten last week and has moved on with his life.

Or so she thought until she set his coffee on his desk and he looked up at her. The heat in his eyes made her tremble. He'd never looked at her like that in the office before.

"Was your family glad to have you back home?"

"My nephews were more interested in what I brought them," she answered. "Lynette and Chuck agreed that I looked tanned and rested, which, according to them, was just what I needed."

He nodded thoughtfully and straightened in his chair. "I'd like to meet them sometime."

"My family?" She had to be mistaken. That couldn't be what he meant.

"Yes."

"Oh."

"Have lunch with me today and we can discuss it."

"I, uh, generally eat lunch at my desk."

"Not today."

"Is this business-related?"

His frown deepened. "Of course not."

"Then don't issue orders about my personal time." She turned and went back to her desk. She started filing papers and folders, her back to his door.

After several minutes she heard Dean clear his throat. She looked over her shoulder and saw him standing beside her desk.

"What do you need?" she asked pleasantly.

"Some manners. Obviously. I apologize for ordering you around."

"Apology accepted."

"I, uh, I'd like to take you to lunch. Please?"

She shut the file drawer and walked over to him. "I don't think that's a good idea. I enjoyed the trip and appreciate your giving me the opportunity to get away from the cold weather for a few days. Now that we're back at work, I believe it would be better if we return to our regular routine."

"I don't see what's wrong with having lunch together."

"At the moment the office staff is under the impression I decided to take off a week while you were gone. Once they see us together and notice our tans, they'll figure out we were together."

"Do you care?"

"Yes."

"Why?"

"I don't want to become the stereotypical secretary who's seeing her boss socially."

"I'm not suggesting we date. It's no big deal to have lunch at the same time, is it?"

"You're being deliberately obtuse."

"No, I'm not. I prefer to think of myself as unconsciously obtuse."

"I'd rather not go out today," she said politely. "I plan to study over my lunch hour. I brought a sandwich."

He nodded slowly. "You're probably right," he said.

She picked up some papers and turned away to the filing cabinet.

Jodie waited until he'd returned to his desk and then rested her forehead against the filing cabinet. She hoped he hadn't noticed that she was trembling. His attitude had caught her off guard.

If she consistently turned him down, he would soon give up and get on with his life, which was just the way she wanted things. She knew his dating patterns. The last thing she needed or wanted was to become involved with him.

And…if she repeated that often enough, she might be able to convince herself.

Dean sat down at his desk and looked at the work awaiting him. Most of it was to approve what had been done in his absence and to sign off on it. He leaned back in his chair and swung around to face the windows.

Jodie was right. Of course she was. Just because he'd enjoyed her company this past week didn't give him the right to expect their relationship to continue in the same way here in Chicago.

She was his secretary. That's all. The thought reminded him that he needed to call Frank. He'd leave her alone. They'd probably get back to their routine all right if he could forget how much he'd enjoyed kissing her and seeing her in a swimsuit. How much he'd enjoyed their conversations.

He shook his head to clear it. Getting emotional about the trip was ridiculous. Dean turned back to his desk and reached for his private address book. Now that he was no longer seeing Rachel, he knew of several women he could call. He only had to pick one.

He reached for the phone.

That night Dean's home phone rang close to eleven o'clock. He glanced at the caller ID and shook his head.

"Hello, Rachel," he said when he picked up the phone.

"Oh! There you are. I've been looking for you all week. Your office said you were out of town, and when I asked to speak to Jodie, I was told she'd taken a week off, so there was no way I could think of to reach you."

"Well, now you've found me. Did you find something else of mine that I left at your place?"

"Oh, honey, I am so sorry for the way I treated you. I don't blame you for not returning my calls. I don't usually behave so atrociously. It was just a really bad day for me."

"I noticed."

"Please forgive me. I miss you so much." She lowered her voice. "I've missed making love to you."

He thought about the relationship he'd had with Rachel and realized that he'd put her completely out of his mind. That told him what he needed to know where she was concerned. Whatever they'd had, it was over.

"Did you remember that this is the weekend we were going up to Wisconsin to visit Winnie and Fred?"

"Rachel, I figured that when you broke up with me, we wouldn't be seeing each other again, much less Winnie and Fred."

"I was awful and I know I was. But I didn't mean any of it. I was just angry and I took it out on you."

"As I recall, I was the reason you were angry."

"Well…but that doesn't matter in the larger scheme of things. Let's face it, all couples quarrel. That's the first one we've had in the three months we've been seeing each other."

He didn't say anything.

"Dean?"

"I'm sorry, Rachel, but I've already made plans for the weekend."

"What sort of plans?" she asked suspiciously.

"Nothing you'd be interested in."

"Try me," she said flatly.

"I have a date Saturday evening with someone I've known for a long while. You don't know her."

"You're seeing someone else!" Her voice lost its rounded tones.

"You made it quite clear you never wanted to see me again. I took you at your word."

"I said I was sorry," she wailed. "Please don't do this to me!"

"Rachel, listen to me. There's no reason to continue seeing each other. The points you made were valid. If it took your getting angry to tell me, then so be it. I'm not going to change, you know. You were right. I am married to my work. I forget social events. I'm bad about escorting you to everything you want to attend. Why bother to continue to see me? There are lots of men who would be eager to spend time with you."

She didn't reply right away. When she did, she sounded

as if she might be crying. "I screwed up. I know that. I know your work is important to you. I was way out of line that night and I know it. I just want to see you once in a while."

"I'll call you when I can, but I picked up a new client last week and I'll be putting in long hours coming up with the right combination of security devices to protect his company." He thought about their situation for a moment. "I'll give you a call in the next week or two. Have fun with Fred and Winnie."

He hung up the phone and wandered over to the windows. His condo had a great view of Lake Michigan. As a rule he found the sight relaxing. Tonight he felt lonely, which was most unusual.

He went into his bedroom, undressed and stretched out on the bed.

He was doing what needed to be done. He'd see Susan Saturday night and catch up on her news. They'd lost touch after he'd moved his mother into the nursing home. Susan had been her live-in caregiver and a sweet woman. He'd been surprised that she hadn't remarried by this time. She'd been a widow for six years or more.

As for Rachel...he'd have to think about whether he wanted to spend much time with her. He discovered that although he was lonely, Rachel wasn't the answer. He refused to consider who might be.

Jodie's phone was ringing when she walked into her office the next morning. She dropped her purse on the desk and reached for the phone.

"This is Jodie."

"Hi, Jodie. It's me...Rachel."

"Oh. Good morning. I'm not sure if Dean's here yet. Do you want me to have him call you?"

"Oh, no! No. I, uh, I called to talk to you."

"Really?"

"Yes. You know, Jodie, I admire you a great deal and I know that Dean couldn't get along without you."

When Rachel paused, Jodie didn't know what to say. What was this phone call about?

Finally Rachel said, "I mean, I know you're discreet and I'd rather you not tell Dean that I called."

"All right."

"The thing is that Dean and I had a spat a week or so ago and I think he's still a little angry with me. He didn't return my calls last week, and when I spoke to him last night, he said he was seeing someone else."

Well, of course he was. Dean Logan didn't waste time. He must have found someone who would have lunch with him or was available for whatever else he wanted. Good.

"I see."

"He's just trying to make me jealous and he wouldn't tell me who he was seeing. Do you know?"

"I have no idea."

"Oh." Rachel sounded disappointed. "He said he'd known her for a long time. I thought you'd probably know her."

Jodie chuckled. "He knows so many people that I wouldn't be able to guess. After all, he's lived in Chicago for years."

"Oh, he'll probably tell me," Rachel finally said with a laugh. "Once he's over his anger. We were supposed to visit some friends in northern Wisconsin this weekend, but I guess he's planning to see her instead."

"I'm sorry, Rachel. I know this must be painful for you."

Rachel sighed. "It's my fault. I must have been going through PMS or something and took it out on him."

"I hope the two of you can work it out," Jodie said. She was sincere. It would be easier for her to have him completely unavailable.

"Thanks for listening, Jodie. I appreciate it."

Jodie hung up, dropped her purse in the drawer and peeked around the corner into Dean's office. It was empty. Thank goodness. She doubted that he'd appreciate her discussing him with Rachel, although in the past she and Rachel had talked to each other regularly.

The next time the phone rang, it was Dean.

"Hi, sorry I didn't let you know I wouldn't be in this morning. Something came up that I needed to take care of."

"No problem. Believe it or not, your phone has been quiet. Maybe everybody thinks you're still on vacation."

"Good. I should be in around two o'clock."

"Okay."

As soon as she hung up the phone, the intercom buzzed. It was Betty.

"Your secret admirer has left something for you at my desk."

"I'm sure. I don't have a secret admirer."

"Well, someone just sent you a beautiful bouquet of tropical flowers. They look and smell heavenly. He must be in looove." She drawled the last word.

What was Lynette up to now?

When Jodie walked into the reception area, she found a truly awesome vase filled with lush flowers. "Was there a card?" she asked.

"Don't know," Betty replied.

Jodie looked through the long stems and saw a small white card. She opened the envelope and stared at the message.

Thought you'd enjoy the scent of the islands in your office. D

"Well?" Betty asked brightly.

"Oh! A friend from school."

"No kidding. Have you been seeing him long?"

She looked at the flowers before answering Betty. "I've known him for years."

Jodie carried the large vase back to her office and placed it on top of the filing cabinet. The flowers smelled enchanting, and she wished she knew what Dean Logan was up to.

Nine

When Jodie arrived at Lynette's on Friday, she realized they had company. She stopped in the hallway to hang up her coat. As soon as she walked into the living room, Chuck said, "Look who's in town," motioning to Carl Grantham, who was sitting across from him.

"Carl! What a surprise. What brings you to Chicago at this time of year?"

Carl got up and hugged her. He'd been Chuck's best man at their wedding, and as the maid of honor, Jodie had spent time with him. He was a great guy. He was also gay, which she considered to be a loss to the female population.

"The company sent me. I tried to convince them that Florida would have been better, but they wouldn't listen to me."

Carl could have been a model had he wanted, but he preferred being an engineer.

"How long are you going to be here?" she asked.

"Until Tuesday. Chuck and Lynette insisted I stay here with them. I told them I could get a hotel since it was a business expense, but…" He shrugged his shoulders.

"I know. I've never been able to win an argument with Chuck either, and you've known him longer than I have!"

Chuck chimed in. "We've got a lot to catch up on. The guest bedroom is far enough away from the kids that he won't be disturbed by them."

Lynette came in from the kitchen. "Hi, sweetie," she said to Jodie, giving her a hug. "You're just in time to help me get the food on the table."

"Where are the boys?"

"They're spending the night with Chuck's folks, and Emily is asleep. I won't guarantee for how long, though, so let's eat."

Over dinner Carl told them what was going on in New York and discussed some of the plays he'd seen. His partner was an actor who was presently in one of the popular musicals on Broadway.

"I would love to see him onstage sometime," Jodie said. "His voice alone sends chills through me."

"And when did you hear his voice?" Lynette asked with a smile.

"While you guys were on your honeymoon and I called Carl to tell him he'd left his jacket in my car. Carl wasn't there, so Chris and I had a nice long chat."

"Telling tales about me is what they were doing," Carl said with a mock frown.

"As I recall," Chuck said, "he was touring when we got married and couldn't come to the wedding."

Carl nodded. "He'd just gotten in when Jodie called."

"I didn't see the coat in the backseat for several days. It had fallen to the floor."

"I was wondering if the three of you would like to see the musical showing at the McCormick. I saw it on Broadway and it's really good."

Lynette shook her head. "As much as I'd like to, I can't ask Chuck's folks to keep the boys two nights in a row."

"Which is an excuse," Chuck said. "She doesn't want to leave Emily with anyone."

"Well, that's true."

Carl looked at Jodie. "How about you?"

"I'd love to! I haven't gone to the theatre in much too long a time."

"Great. I'll see about tickets for tomorrow night. If they're sold out, we can catch the Sunday matinee—that is, if you're available."

"I think I can safely say that my social calendar is quite bare either day."

Carl shook his head. "Then the men around here are blind. You look sensational. Where did you get the tan? The contrast with your blond hair and blue eyes is stunning."

"I was in Hawaii last week."

"Alone?" he asked with a lifted brow.

She glanced at Lynette and Chuck. "Well, not exactly."

"Aha."

"No, no, nothing like that. I was with my boss who had business there."

"He must be eighty years old not to have been aware of you."

Jodie laughed and knew she was blushing. "He's a businessman, completely wrapped up in his company." She refused to look at Lynette. Instead she kept her eyes trained on Carl.

After dinner the men went into the other room while Jodie and Lynette cleaned up the kitchen. Jodie was putting dishes in the dishwasher when Lynette said, "I have a question. You don't have to answer it, but did Dean make a pass at you while you were there?"

Jodie took her time straightening and turning to face Lynette. "A pass?" she repeated, stalling for time.

"You know...did he try to kiss you or suggest you could be more than a secretary to him? I couldn't help but notice that you blush every time he's mentioned, which has never been your reaction to him before." She studied Jodie's face. "You're right. It's none of my business. You're a grown woman and I don't need to hover." She touched Jodie's cheek. "I just don't want to see you hurt."

"There's nothing going on between us," Jodie answered truthfully. "He's all business at the office. Nothing's changed. He's already dating someone else."

"Doesn't take him long, does it?"

"I'm sure they're lined up waiting for him to notice them."

They walked into the living room and Jodie turned to Carl. "I need to get home. Call me when you have the tickets."

"Even if we don't get the tickets for tomorrow night, I'd like to take you to dinner."

"I'd like that."

"Good."

"I'll draw you a map to her place," Chuck said. "She's moved since you were here last."

"Great," Jodie said. "I'll wait to hear from you."

Jodie drove home thinking about the evening. She thought the world of Carl. He was drop-dead handsome with a wry sense of humor, graduated at the top of his class at MIT, but most important, he was a warm, gracious person.

Nothing like Dean, who had returned to being a bear this past week, growling at whoever was closest, which was usually her.

The oddest thing, though. He'd sent her a dozen roses today. When she'd thanked him, he'd nodded without looking up and said, "I noticed the others were fading. It's nice to have fresh flowers in the office."

So the flowers weren't really for her. They were for the office.

Once home, Jodie went to bed. While waiting for sleep, she wondered what Dean was doing tonight.

Dean sat at his desk at home and read contracts that had been prepared for new clients. With all the security breaches in the corporate world these days, more and more companies were looking for high-tech solutions, causing his business to flourish. So why wasn't he more excited about the increase?

Was it possible he was bored?

Of course not. That would never happen.

It was almost midnight before he went to bed. Despite the hour, he had trouble falling asleep.

Carl had managed to get tickets for the Saturday-night performance. He picked Jodie up early enough for them to have dinner before the show.

As soon as she opened the door, he said, "You look fabulous, Ms. Cameron."

"Come in, Carl. You look stunning yourself."

"Stunning?" He quirked his eyebrow.

"You look like you should be modeling. Custom-made suit?"

He nodded. "So. Are we ready to go?"

"Absolutely." She put on her coat, picked up her purse and joined him at the door.

By the time they reached the theater, Jodie had laughed so much her tears had wiped off the little makeup she wore. Not that she cared. She couldn't remember the last time she'd so enjoyed herself.

With Dean perhaps?

Don't go there.

Once they were seated, she said, "I can't believe you got such good seats."

"Actually they were a last-minute cancellation. Looks as if we lucked out."

As the lights began to dim, Jodie noticed a couple being seated a few rows in front of them. She recognized the man immediately—it was Dean with his new girlfriend.

She couldn't believe that they had chosen the same night to see the musical. She gave her head a quick shake of dismissal.

"Something wrong?" Carl leaned toward her to ask.

"Not really. I just saw the man I work for. He doesn't seem to be the musical-theater kind, so I was a little surprised." She nodded toward the couple.

"How long have you worked for him?"

"Close to five years. It's a great company to work for.

They've paid for me to take college courses at night. I'll actually get my degree this spring."

"Great benefits."

She watched as Dean leaned over and said something to the woman he was with. She looked to be about his age, and from what Jodie could see, she appeared to be very attractive.

The overture finished and the curtains opened. After that, Jodie forgot everything else but the magical experience of musical theater.

Dean and Susan went into the lobby during intermission. He told her to wait there and he'd get them something to drink from the bar. While going through the crowd, he almost literally ran into Jodie.

"Well, hi," he said with a slight smile. "Fancy meeting you here."

"Hello, Dean," she said. "I'd like you to meet Carl Grantham."

Dean hadn't realized that she was with someone. He held out his hand. "Dean Logan." The man was everything he wasn't. Good-looking—all right, great-looking—debonair and appeared charming.

"Dean is the man I work for," she said to Carl.

"I'm glad to meet you. Jodie was singing your praises a little earlier."

Dean looked at Jodie and she turned a fiery red. He looked back at Carl. "That's always good to hear. If you'll excuse me, I was headed to the bar to get drinks for Susan and me. Good meeting you, Carl. I'll see you at the office, Jodie."

Dean turned his back and walked away before he did or said something outrageous. He wanted to flatten Carl and grab Jodie, proclaiming that she belonged to him and only to him. He'd never experienced such a surge of jealousy and possessiveness. What was wrong with him anyway? He'd never dated Jodie, so why should a few shared kisses last week make him feel so possessive of her, of all people? He wasn't jealous of women he dated.

Dean glanced back at the couple, who appeared to be enjoying each other's company. He frowned. Damn it, he didn't want her seeing other men. When he rejoined Susan, she thanked him and said, "What a striking couple you stopped and talked to. They look perfect for each other. Are they married?"

"No. She's my secretary."

"I see. Jodie, isn't it?"

"You've got a great memory. Yes, that's Jodie Cameron."

"I remember when you hired her. After a few months you couldn't say enough good things about her."

"Well, she's taking another position in the company in a week or so and I'm going to need another secretary. Don't suppose you'd be interested?"

Susan laughed. "I'm afraid not. I'm more comfortable doing private care work."

"How do you like your present assignment?"

"I like it. In fact, the son of the man I'm caring for has shown an interest in me."

"That's not surprising. The question is, are you encouraging him?"

"I believe I am," she admitted with a smile. "He's a single parent with two children. I have no idea where their mother is. She's never mentioned. The girls and I get along famously. They were upset that I was going out tonight with someone other than their dad."

"A ready-made family. Is that what you want?"

Tears filled her eyes. "That's the only way I'll have children. I think this could turn into something serious." She blinked away the tears. "I don't think he was particularly enamored of my seeing you either."

"It will do him good. We won't tell him that you're the sister I never had—"

"And the brother I never had," she finished.

He touched her cheek. "You know I'll always be there for you. Would you like me to meet him and make intimidating noises about his treating you right or he'll answer to me?"

Susan laughed out loud and gave him a hug. "I really don't think that will be necessary, but I'll keep it in mind."

Jodie watched the attractive woman with Dean hug him and turned away. The lights flickered, signaling that it was time to return for the next act. Once seated, Jodie did her best not to watch for Dean.

She also decided that she didn't need to see him with other women either. Next time she'd make certain not to go anywhere where she might run into him.

Ten

There was another bouquet of flowers on her desk when Jodie arrived at work on Monday. This time she didn't bother to thank him since the flowers were for the office. However, she did comment on how beautiful they were.

He looked up from his work. "Did you enjoy the musical?" he asked.

"Very much. I haven't seen a stage production in much too long a time. How about you?"

He shrugged. "It was okay, I guess. If you like that sort of thing. I've never been able to figure out why, when they become romantic, they sing to each other instead of kissing."

She smiled. "So why did you go?"

"Susan mentioned wanting to see it."

"She seems very nice."

He leaned back in his chair and studied her. "I spoke to

Frank earlier. He said he could put you to work in three weeks if that's okay with you."

She nodded. "That's fine with me. I'll call the employment agency and find someone to replace me."

He cleared his throat. "Jodie, there's no one who can replace you. I'd like to keep you here, but I know I'm being selfish. You deserve a chance to put your education to good use and I don't want to hold you back."

She blinked back the tears that suddenly appeared. "Thank you for giving me the chance. I promise I'll find someone who is every bit as good as I am. Within a week you won't notice there's been a change."

He shook his head. "That will never happen." He picked up a letter lying on his desk, a clear dismissal of her, which was just as well.

Jodie returned to her desk. She was going to miss seeing him every day, but it was better this way. The infatuation she seemed to have acquired while on Maui would die a natural death once she wasn't around him so often.

The days went by and Jodie slowly settled into a routine of doing her work and interviewing prospective employees.

Rachel seemed to be back in Dean's life. She called him every day or so, and Jodie happened to hear him making plans with her for a weekend next month.

Jodie spent her evenings working on school projects and studying for finals. She'd be glad when she moved to her new position. Being around the old Dean who never laughed and rarely smiled made her heart ache for him. He'd returned to his hard-crusted shell, and it was as though the man she'd gotten to know in Hawaii no longer existed.

She had hoped that, for his sake, he would look around him and enjoy his life more fully. It was his choice, of course, to revert back to the all-business-all-the-time man he'd been.

Why should she care?

She didn't want to think about the answer.

Sunday turned out to be almost springlike, which wasn't surprising considering that spring would be there in another few weeks. Jodie decided to go jogging. She hadn't been out much these past several weeks. She drove to one of the nearby parks, parked, stretched and started out in a slow jog.

She recognized some of the other joggers because they'd been coming there for years. The sunshine and blue sky must have encouraged them to get out, just as it had her.

Afterward, she stopped into a deli and bought a large sandwich and headed home.

She decided to shower before eating. She'd barely gotten wet when she heard the doorbell. Since Lynette always called first, she didn't have a clue who could be there.

Jodie hurriedly stepped out of the shower and grabbed a bath towel, then hurried to the door.

"Who is it?"

"Dean."

"Dean?" She panicked. "Hold on a sec." She rushed into the bedroom and found a robe to put on and hurried back to open the door. "I'm sorry to keep you waiting. I was in the shower when I heard the bell. Please. Come in."

He walked in and said, "I hope you don't mind my stopping by without calling first."

"I'll forgive you this once," she replied with a smile, "especially since I just got home and you wouldn't have reached me anyway. Would you like some coffee while I get dressed?"

He shook his head. "Had too much already, but thanks."

She waved at the grouping of sofa and chairs and said, "Have a seat. I'll be right back."

Jodie hurried into her bedroom and closed the door. What was he doing there? And why was she letting his presence rattle her so? She didn't have any answers. She dug out an old pair of jeans and a faded sweatshirt, stuck her feet in house slippers and went back to the living room.

He stood as soon as he saw her. "You look comfortably casual," he said with a lopsided grin.

"I am." She stood there for a moment, waiting, and when he didn't say anything, she said, "Let's sit down. I'm sure you have a reason for coming by."

He settled back on the sofa while she sat on the edge of one of her chairs.

"I've been thinking."

That sounded a little ominous. "About what?"

"Us."

She frowned. "There isn't an us."

"Actually there is, whether we do anything about it or not. We became friends while we were in Maui. I'd like to give the relationship a chance and see where it takes us."

Oh, dear. His reason for being there was worse than she'd thought.

After a moment she replied, "I don't think so."

"Why not?"

She rolled her eyes. "Oh, let me count the ways. One, I

work for you, which we've already discussed. Nothing has changed in that regard. Two, I'm not into flings. Besides, you're still involved with Rachel and I don't want to get in the middle of that."

He looked uncomfortable. "We've agreed that the relationship isn't working for either of us. I won't be seeing her anymore."

"I can't imagine her breaking up with you unless she found out you're seeing someone else, and I don't believe that's the case. I always know when you're seeing someone. You send them flowers, you get them tickets…" Her voice trailed off and she stared at him in dismay. "You sent *me* flowers."

"So I did."

She stared at him, feeling confused. "Well…but…you didn't mean them in that way," she said.

"I meant them exactly that way," he murmured.

"Oh, my gosh."

"You didn't guess?"

"Are you kidding? Of course I didn't think that's what they meant." She couldn't believe she was having this conversation with Dean.

He leaned forward, resting his elbows on his knees. "The thing is, Jodie, I'd like to start seeing you socially. I discovered that I enjoy your company. When I'm with you, I see everything through your eyes and I like the new perspective." He kept his gaze focused on her. "Teach me how to relax and enjoy life a little more, like we did in Hawaii."

"You're asking me to tutor you?" she asked, frowning slightly.

"If you want to call it that."

"For how long?"

"I don't understand the question."

"Well, let me put it this way. How long do you generally date one person before moving on?"

"What kind of question is that? I have no idea."

"Well, I do. It averages about two to two and a half months. How long do you expect to see me?"

He threw up his hands. "This isn't the conversation I thought I'd be having."

She crossed her arms. "Really? Did you think I'd rush into your arms when you decided you want to spend time with me away from the office?"

"If I did, that idea got blown out of the water."

"Dean?"

"What?"

"What's this all about?"

He leaned back on the sofa, rested his head against the back and sighed.

"I miss you more than I could have dreamed I would. We were good together. We had fun together. Or I did, at least. What's wrong with extending that?"

"We could try it, I suppose," she said thoughtfully.

"Your enthusiasm is underwhelming."

"I could be your transition person until you find someone else."

He closed his eyes. "Transition person," he repeated without inflection.

"Maybe we could do that. Still nothing serious."

He straightened. "So you'll do it?"

"Within reason. I'm busy with school, as you know, but maybe once a week or so we could spend some time together." She brightened. "We could meet for coffee after my classes. Have dinner on weekends. Is that what you want?"

"Never mind what I want. I'll take what I can get."

"All right then." She stood up. "I brought home a sandwich from the deli. I'm willing to share it if you're hungry."

"As a matter of fact, my appetite is definitely returning." He stood, putting him a step or two away from her. "Shall we seal our agreement with a kiss?"

She looked wary. "We were talking about food."

"Of course. Why don't I take you out for lunch? It's a beautiful day for this early in the year. We might take a drive after we eat." He lifted her chin with his forefinger. "Just know that food isn't the only cause of my hunger," he said and kissed her.

Not fair, not fair at all. He knew how his kisses affected her. There had been too many occasions when he'd felt her reaction.

This kiss was no exception, even though she stiffened at first, determined not to be swayed. It was his gentleness that destroyed her resolve, because she'd never considered him a gentle person until they'd spent the week together.

Now all the emotions he evoked within her poured out and she knew they were more powerful than her determination not to succumb.

The problem was that all her valid reasons still stood.

The problem was that she found him too compelling to resist spending a little more time with him.

The problem was that she was going to be hurt badly when the relationship ended. All she could do at this point was deal with the pain at that time.

Eleven

The following Wednesday Jodie reached for her purse as she prepared to leave the office when Dean called to her. She went into his office.

Without looking up from the schematic drawing covering most of his desk he asked, "What time are your classes over tonight?"

His question was the first personal remark he'd made to her since he'd left her on Sunday. Jodie had begun to wonder if she'd dreamed that her boss had come over to plead his case for seeing her socially or whether it was some fantasy she'd concocted to relieve an otherwise boring weekend.

"Nine."

"Tell me where to meet you," he said, marking something on the drawing.

"Uh, well, there's a coffeehouse a couple of blocks from—"

"No. I'll pick you up at school. Where are your classes being held?" When she didn't answer, he straightened away from the desk and looked at her. He was still in his boss mode, snapping out orders.

After a moment she gave him the address, turned around and walked out.

Dean watched her leave with a frown. He hadn't handled that right. He wasn't sure what he'd done wrong, but he could tell from the stiffness in her shoulders as she walked away that she wasn't pleased with him.

He rolled his head, trying to loosen the muscles in his neck and shoulders. Women were a mystery he'd never been able to solve. Until now he'd never particularly cared.

Ever since they had returned from Hawaii he'd had a tough time concentrating whenever she was around. He'd been disgusted at himself for not being able to clamp down on his emotions. All she had to do was walk into the room and he immediately wanted to make love to her. He'd been forced to stay behind his desk so that she didn't see his physical response to her.

So he didn't look at her any more than was absolutely necessary.

Not that his idea was much help, since he had a similar reaction whenever he heard her voice.

She was driving him crazy.

The problem was that it was too late to do anything about it. When they'd first returned from Hawaii and she'd refused to have lunch with him, he'd tried to force himself to forget about his attraction to her. He'd only been kidding himself.

Now that he'd finally gotten her to agree to see him, he'd managed to offend her in some way.

Great going, Logan.

When Jodie walked out of the classroom that evening, she saw Dean leaning against the opposite wall, his arms crossed. She did a double take. He looked too much like the man she'd gotten to know in Hawaii, not the man she worked for.

She started toward him at the same time he straightened.

"Hi," she said.

He smiled at her. "Hi, yourself. Ready for some coffee?"

"Sure."

"The weather is nasty. Would you like to go to my place?"

She lifted her brow. "For coffee?"

He looked innocent. "Of course."

"All right."

When they reached the doors of the building, she could see that rain and touches of sleet poured from the sky. He opened an umbrella she hadn't noticed and, pulling her close to his side, hurried her to the car.

"Wow," she said, a little breathless, once they were inside the car.

"Where's your car?"

"At home. I took the bus."

"Good thinking."

She watched the windshield wipers ferociously battle the rain and sleet. "I decided before all of this hit."

"You knew I'd get you home."

"There is that."

She'd never been to his home, although she knew where it was: in one of the high-rise buildings overlooking Lake Michigan. He entered the underground parking area and parked by the elevators in a space with his name and the word *Reserved*.

The elevator silently whisked them to his floor, and by the time he opened the door to his home, all Jodie could think was that she was way out of her league.

He helped her off with her coat and said, "Have a seat. I'll go make coffee."

Jodie wandered over to the windows and looked out at the shimmering lights muted by the rain. If ever she'd needed a reality check, his place did that for her. She remembered how she'd gone on and on about the luxury condo while they were in Hawaii. His home was more luxurious.

She closed her eyes. She would be an idiot to think that he could have more than a passing interest in her.

"Here you go," he said from behind her. Jodie turned and watched him put a tray on the coffee table in front of the long sectional furniture arranged to take in the view.

"What am I doing here?" she asked, walking toward him.

He straightened and looked at her. "Having coffee?"

She gave her head a quick shake. "That isn't what I mean," she replied and sat down on the edge of the sofa. "This isn't going to work."

He sat a couple of feet away from her. "I noticed you seemed to be upset with me when you left the office."

She reached for the coffee. "That was something different," she replied and sipped on the drink. She realized she was shaking, as much from nerves as from the weather. She held the cup with both hands, warming them.

"So what happened to cause you to change your mind in three days?"

She didn't answer him. Instead she continued to carefully drink her coffee.

When she didn't answer, he asked briskly, "Am I supposed to guess?" Now he sounded like the man she worked for.

Jodie set her coffee cup back on the tray and turned to him. The problem was that he didn't look like her boss at the moment. With his hair mussed and in his cable-knit sweater, he reminded her of the man she'd spent time with in Hawaii.

She bit her lip. "I know I said that I'd start seeing you, but the truth is that we come from two different worlds and nothing is going to change that. I live a simple life and have simple tastes. I'm not at all your type."

"What exactly is my type?" he asked, his jaw stiff.

She waved her hand vaguely at the room. "Women who are used to all this luxury, who expect it, women who go to operas and symphonies and are photographed whenever they attend some function. That's not me."

He studied her, looking quizzical. "I don't recall inviting you to an opera or the symphony."

"You know what I mean," she snapped.

"I wish to hell I did. What is going on in that busy brain of yours?"

"I've come to my senses. I can't do this. I'm sorry." She stood. "I need to get home. I'll call a cab."

"Not on your life. You're not going to run away from this discussion."

"Please date someone else instead of me. The woman

you took to the musical, for instance. Or…I don't care. Just someone else."

"I believe your prejudices are showing."

"What are you talking about?"

"You can't go out with me because I attend various functions around town? Or are we back to the fact that you work for me?"

"Actually I do dislike you giving me orders when it's not job-related."

"Care to give me an example?"

"This afternoon. You took charge once I agreed to see you tonight. Told me what you were going to do and where we'd meet."

"You could have said no."

"I could have, yes. I should have."

"I get the sense that we're talking in circles without getting to the crux of what's bothering you."

"All right. Then here it is. Hawaii was wonderful. I couldn't have imagined a more perfect vacation. But the vacation is over. Yes, there's a definite attraction between us. You want to encourage it. I want to ignore it, which is why I'm relieved to be moving into another department next week. Let's forget about Hawaii and get on with our lives."

"I believe we tried that, but I, for one, have found it impossible after getting to know you better."

She closed her eyes. "I can't do this," she said quietly.

The silent room seemed weighted with emotion.

He studied his coffee in silence. When he looked up, his face revealed nothing of what he was thinking or feeling. "I'll drive you home," he said quietly.

Jodie waited until she was alone in her apartment before she broke down and cried.

Jodie moved into the engineering department the next week. Dean had hired one of the women Jodie recommended. Her name was Candace Rudin and she appeared to be quite competent. Jodie had expected to spend several days with her, but Candace had quickly grasped the routine, the filing system and the way Dean liked to work.

Once in Engineering, Jodie was determined to learn everything she could as quickly as possible. Several weeks went by, and Frank praised her repeatedly, patiently answering her questions when she couldn't figure something out.

She had been there two months when Frank dropped an envelope on her desk one morning. She looked up. "It isn't payday, is it?"

He shook his head. "No. It's time you learned firsthand about installing our equipment. That's your plane ticket."

A plane trip. Great. "I don't suppose we could do this somewhere that we could drive to, by any chance?"

"Sorry. Besides, I won't be going. Logan said that since you'd already been to this particular office, it made sense for you to see the next step. He'll be going with you to show you the ropes."

There was only one office she'd visited and it was in Honolulu. She peeked into the envelope and saw the ticket, confirming her suspicions. She looked at Frank. "I haven't finished what I'm working on," she pointed out.

"Doesn't matter since there's no rush on that one. Besides, you'll only be in Hawaii a few days—four at the most."

"Oh." She forced herself to smile. "Well. That's good.

I mean, I'll enjoy being part of the installation process. I'm just surprised that Dean would be the one to do it."

Frank shrugged. "I'll admit he hasn't done an installation in a long while. Probably wants to keep his hand in. Don't worry, though. You already know how he can be and won't be caught off guard when he starts snapping at you for not working fast enough. Just ignore his moods."

"I'll do my best."

Twelve

Dean greeted her briskly when she arrived at the airport the next morning. She had a moment of déjà vu when she saw him, except that today he wore a business suit.

She had also dressed for a business trip, in a light-colored suit and matching heels.

"Good morning," she said, walking up to him.

He turned around. "It's nice to see you again," he replied politely. "Have you checked your bag?"

She nodded.

"Have you had breakfast? If you haven't, there's a restaurant along the concourse where we could get something."

"Fine."

He strode along the corridor, a man on the move, and Jodie had to skip a time or two in order to keep up with him.

Once they found the restaurant, sat down and ordered,

Jodie caught her breath. Her shortness of breath was in no way connected to seeing Dean again. He looked like a modern-day pirate in his dark suit. All he needed was a knife between his teeth.

"How is Candace working out?" she asked during their meal.

"She's all right."

She couldn't think of anything more to say to him. She wanted to ask him why he'd decided to do the installation himself rather than send someone else.

But she didn't.

She wanted to ask him why he'd decided to have her accompany him, given their situation.

But she didn't.

Was it because he wanted to prove to her that he'd moved on after she'd turned him down? Perhaps. No doubt he was already involved with someone else by now.

Which was just as well. She wished that she'd been seeing someone these past few weeks, someone who would have helped her forget about her attraction to him. This trip would be much easier for her if that were the case.

"How do you like working for Frank?" he asked after several minutes of silence.

"He's great. I'm fascinated by all that we're doing."

"You'll be able to see how we implement the work your department does in Furukawa's offices." He paused for a moment. "I thought you might enjoy seeing the islands again."

"Are we going to stay in the condo?"

"No. Candace made reservations for us to stay in one of the hotels in Honolulu."

"Oh."

"Are you ready to go to our gate?"

She nodded.

Once on the concourse, he continued his fast pace until Jodie finally said, "Dean, I can't keep up with you in these heels. Would you please slow down?"

He immediately stopped and waited for her to catch up with him. "Sorry. My mind was on other things."

They continued walking for what seemed forever to Jodie before they reached their gate.

They found seats although the departure lounge was rapidly filling up with passengers waiting to board.

Dean spotted their plane, which they could see through the glass wall. "Looks like they're finishing loading luggage and food." He glanced at his watch. "We should be boarding shortly." When she didn't comment, he asked, "Do you have something to read on the plane?"

"In my purse."

Dean was not usually so talkative. Making idle chitchat wasn't part of his personality.

"Dean?"

"Yes?"

"Look, I know this is awkward for both of us. I appreciate your taking me on this assignment. I know you didn't have to be the one to go."

"Actually I felt that Furukawa needed to know that his security was important to me. We've stayed in touch these past few weeks ironing out the contract and determining exactly what should be installed. The fact that I'll be installing the systems is personally important."

"Will we start this afternoon?"

"Not with the actual work, no. However, we'll go to his office, pay our respects and invite him to dinner if he doesn't have other plans. We'll get started on the installation first thing tomorrow morning. It won't take more than a couple of days if everything goes according to plan."

The flight attendant announced that it was time to board and they stood. Jodie had noticed that once again they were flying first-class.

As soon as she'd found out she'd be making this trip, she'd visited her doctor and asked for something to help her deal with her anxiety about flying. He'd given her a prescription for a mild anti-anxiety drug and told her to take it a half hour before flying. She'd taken it with breakfast and was already feeling calmer.

Dean escorted her to their seats. "Would you prefer to sit on the aisle?" he asked.

"Yes, please."

She reached for the airline magazine in the pocket in front of her and began to read.

"Are you okay about flying?" he asked.

"I think so. Yes."

She could tell that he didn't believe her. It didn't matter. She needed to get used to flying now that she was a representative of the company.

By the time they took off, she was getting sleepy. She'd had a restless night, dreading spending time with Dean again. Lack of sleep, together with the prescription drug, had her yawning by the time they leveled off.

Jodie leaned her seat back and went to sleep.

Dean took the opportunity to study her—the way her mouth was shaped, her thick lashes, the slight tilt of her nose. He'd missed seeing her each day. When he found himself going to her department in hopes of seeing her, he knew he had it bad.

His dreams were filled with her…talking with her, making love to her, riding in the car with her. He was never alone in his dreams now, which was tough when he woke up each morning to discover he *was* alone and none of it was real.

Dean couldn't figure out what was going on with him. Was it because he hadn't been with a woman since the first trip to Hawaii? He hadn't been interested enough in Rachel to respond to her sexual overtures, which was the major reason she knew their relationship had come to an end.

They'd spent a weekend together, a last-ditch effort on her part to prove something to him—or herself. Despite all her attempts at seducing him—provocative night wear, a full-body massage—nothing had worked.

He figured he'd been too tired that weekend. His dreams of Jodie were more satisfying than the reality of being with Rachel.

This trip was to prove something to himself—to prove that his fantasies of Jodie were absurd. Candace had booked a suite so that each of them had a bedroom. They wouldn't be spending much time there.

This was strictly a business trip.

He was not lusting after her.

What he needed to do was find someone nice to date—someone with blond hair and blue eyes, someone who looked trim and fit, someone who was fun to talk to, to be with, someone who could make him laugh.

Someone like Jodie.

* * *

Dean had awakened her as they'd approached Los Angeles. There had been little time for them to find their gate for the next leg of the journey and neither one of them had said very much.

Once they'd been back on the plane, Jodie had read a little but fallen asleep within the first hour. Consequently she felt rested and ready to go to work when they landed in Honolulu.

They checked in to their hotel and she discovered that they had a gorgeous view from the balcony off the main room. Their bedrooms were located on opposite sides of this room.

They met Steve Furukawa at his office and showed him the schematics for the job. Dean answered his questions at length, and when Steve was fully satisfied, they set up a time to begin the next morning.

Steve agreed to have dinner with them, but Jodie begged off. Once Dean left their hotel room, she changed into more casual clothes and took a long, contemplative walk along the beach.

She had to face a difficult fact: she was in love with Dean Logan. She wasn't certain when it had happened, but there was no doubt about it. Being with him again had taught her that she'd been kidding herself when she'd decided she was over her infatuation with him. Of course, she had no intention of acting on her desire for him. She wasn't that stupid or self-destructive.

She wondered if there was a group somewhere she could attend to learn how to get over him. If so, she would definitely join.

By the time she returned to the hotel, the exercise had worked its charm. She was pleasantly tired, tired enough— she hoped—to be able to sleep, since tomorrow would be a long day.

When Jodie opened the door to the suite, she was surprised to see that Dean was there. He was on the balcony, sitting on one chair, his feet propped on another, sipping a drink.

"How was dinner?" she asked, walking over to him.

He moved his feet and motioned for her to sit down. "The food was good and I enjoyed getting to know Steve a little better. He gave me a brief family history. He told me how his family came to Hawaii from Japan many years ago. He's an interesting man."

She sat down and propped her bare feet on the railing. "There's something about this place that seems almost magical. The scent of flowers, the soft breeze. It's easy to forget there's another world out there."

"I watched you walk along the edge of the water. I was relieved to spot you. I was worried when I discovered you weren't here when I got back."

"I had no idea you would return so soon."

"Steve wanted to get home to his family. I enjoyed listening to his stories about his sons and daughters. He's very proud of them."

"You constantly surprise me," she replied.

"In what way?"

"Somehow I can't picture you listening to stories about children."

"Why not?"

She shrugged. "I can't see you as a family man." When he didn't reply, she added, "I didn't mean to offend you."

"I'm not offended. I never thought of myself in that light, so I suppose you're right."

They stayed on the balcony enjoying the night air for a while. Then Dean said, "I'm going to bed. See you in the morning." He stood and stretched, and Jodie straightened and got up, as well.

Once inside, Dean switched off the lamp, leaving the room bathed in moonlight.

"Thank you for giving me this opportunity, Dean."

"No problem. I seem to get some masochistic pleasure whenever I'm around you."

"What do you mean?"

"Don't pretend you don't know, Jodie. I want to make love to you so badly I constantly ache with it. And that's when you're not around."

She hoped the darkness hid her flushed face and the trembling of her body. "I didn't know," she said faintly.

"Do you want a demonstration?" he asked. He walked over to her and drew her into his arms. His kiss was gentle at first. If he'd grabbed her, she could have easily pushed away from him. It was his gentleness that undid her.

The kiss quickly heated up and Jodie felt him pressed against her, his arousal very evident.

Alarms went off in her head...or were they bells? She couldn't tell and at the moment did not care. She slipped her arms around his neck and kissed him back with all the pent-up love and passion she had for him.

Dean was the one who broke away. "I'm sorry. That was inexcusable." He turned and strode toward his bedroom. "Good night."

Good night?

He had kissed the living daylights out of her and all he could say was good night?

Every nerve in her body tingled with anticipation. She took deep, steadying breaths, shaking so hard she could barely stand there. How dare he start something he didn't intend to finish.

She should be grateful.

She should be thankful for his restraint.

She turned away and started to her bedroom and then wheeled around and marched across the room to his closed door. Without knocking, she shoved the door open. She didn't see him but she knew he was there.

"That was a rotten trick, Dean Logan! How dare you start something and then walk away as though nothing had happened!"

She slammed the door and marched back to her room, slamming that door for good measure.

The nerve of the man. Just because she refused to date him. Just because she knew that making love to him would be the worst possible thing she could do to herself didn't mean that she could just walk away after the passionate kiss they'd just shared.

So maybe she did want a fling after all! That was all that Dean would ever have with her.

She went into the bathroom and took off her clothes. She'd take a shower until she was calmer.

She turned on the shower and, without waiting for it to warm up, stepped inside, needing the shock of cold water on her heated body. She stood with the spray hitting her face, forcing herself to let go of her frustration and get a hold on her emotions.

Which was why she didn't hear Dean enter the room until the shower door opened behind her and Dean stepped inside wearing nothing but a smile.

Thirteen

Too bad he didn't have a camera to catch the expression on Jodie's face when she saw him.

"You're right, as usual," he said smoothly. "A gentleman should never, ever start something he doesn't intend to finish." He took the washcloth out of her nerveless fingers and said, "Turn around and I'll scrub your back for you."

She looked down at him and blinked. If she thought he hadn't been affected by that kiss—which he felt certain was quite apparent at the time—she could have no doubt about his condition now.

"Dean?" Her voice sounded strangled as he gently turned her away from him. He traced her spine with his finger from the nape of her neck down to her luscious derriere.

"Yes?"

"What are you doing?"

"Isn't it obvious? Scrubbing your back." He took his time sliding the cloth up and down her spine, pausing at her hips to place his hands on either side.

"That isn't what I—" She stopped and dropped her chin to her chest.

"I never want to leave a woman angry at me for not finishing what I started."

She slowly turned and looked at him.

He smiled at her.

"We're really going to do this, aren't we?" she whispered, her breath catching.

He dropped the cloth and cupped his hands around her face. She really was adorable. "Yes, we really are," he replied…and touched her lips with his tongue. Her mouth was lush and smooth to his touch. He settled his mouth over hers, fighting to control his passion until she was as ready as he was.

If he could.

She placed her hands tentatively on his chest and leaned closer, her mouth opening to him like a rosebud blossoming.

He dropped his hands and stepped back, breathing hard. "I think our shower is over, don't you?"

She looked at him and nodded. Dean reached around her and turned off the water. He led her out of the shower, picked up a towel and quickly dried her off. He swiped the towel over himself, dropped it and picked her up.

She leaned her head against his shoulder, closed her eyes and sighed.

He placed her on his bed, slid the covers from beneath her and yanked them off the bed before he lay down beside her.

"I brought protection," he whispered and nodded toward the bedside table. Her eyes widened at the number he'd brought with him. He grinned. "Just in case," he said.

He kissed her again while he explored the curves and hollows of her body with his hands. He wanted to memorize every inch of her. She shifted and reached for him.

Dean quickly caught her hand. "No fair. This is for you, not me." He trailed kisses along her jaw, down her neck, and touched her nipple with his tongue.

She groaned and he glanced up to see her face. Her eyes were closed and her face was flushed, but it was the soft smile of pleasure that encouraged him. He pulled her gently into his mouth while he played with the other tip, then eventually shifted his mouth to her other one, his hand gliding over her stomach and abdomen until it rested in her nest of blond curls.

Jodie pushed against his hand in invitation and he moved downward, feeling her moist heat. Dean shifted and knelt between her legs. She reached for him, and he took her hands in his before he lowered his head and kissed her curls.

She jumped as though she'd been electrocuted, and he murmured soothing words to her while he explored. She quickly climaxed, crying out, and Dean moved over her, sliding deep inside.

Jodie hugged him to her and fell into the slow rhythm that was costing him a great deal. His body hummed with urgency and he finally gave up all pretense of control. They moved together, uttering soft sounds and breathing heavily.

When she tightened around him in a spasmodic rhythm,

he quickly climaxed with her and, in one final lunge, buried himself deeply inside.

He collapsed on his elbows, careful not to put much weight on her, before he rolled onto the pillow next to hers.

They lay there on the bed without speaking, catching their breaths.

Finally Jodie murmured a soft, "Wow."

He turned his head and gazed at her. "At the very least," he replied.

She turned onto her side and stared at him, which made him a little nervous.

"What are you thinking?" he finally asked as the silence went on.

"My brain shut off much earlier this evening," she replied.

He got up and went into the bathroom, wondering if she was already regretting their intimacy.

Jodie watched the bathroom door close behind Dean, forcing herself to face what had happened just now, what she had triggered by her earlier remarks.

If she'd given the matter much thought, she would have known that Dean would be wonderful in bed. When it came right down to it, she realized now, she'd expected sex. What she'd experienced with him was making love.

A little later he opened the door and peered out. "Want to try that shower again?"

She smiled. "All right."

Despite the fact that he'd seen all there was, she felt shy. She slipped her robe around her.

When she reached him, he immediately removed the robe before cupping her breasts in his hands. He kissed each one and looked at her quizzically. "This isn't what I expected."

"What is that?"

"I want you just as badly now as I did before."

She glanced down at him. "So I see."

He moved reluctantly away and turned on the shower. "However, I don't want you to think I'm some kind of animal." He held out his hand and guided her into the shower.

She took the washcloth and carefully soaped him, enjoying his reaction as she slid her hand along his hardened length. Eventually she soaped his back, as well, discovering the view was equally enticing on that side.

When he rinsed off, he quickly covered her with suds and as quickly rinsed her off before he slid his arms beneath her hips and lifted her, guiding her legs around his waist.

The position left her open to him, and he slipped inside her, leaning her back against the wall.

She closed her eyes, her arms around his neck, and gave herself up to the experience.

"Jodie?"

"Hmm?"

"We need to get up. It's almost six."

Her eyelids flew open. "Already? How did that happen? I feel as though I just fell asleep."

"Probably because you did. I'm afraid I kept you awake most of the night." He rolled out of bed and walked to the door. "If we hurry, we can get something to eat before we go to work."

Jodie wasted no time getting out of bed once he closed the door behind him. She quickly dressed, dismayed that her hair stood out everywhere. That's what she got for going to bed with wet hair. She shook her head at herself. Her hair was the last thing she'd been thinking of last night.

She did what she could with it, forcing it back into a tidy bun, and prayed that her hair would not give her trouble today, of all days.

Dean was waiting in the sitting area when she walked out of the bedroom. He wore a sports jacket and slacks, his shirt collar open.

They decided to eat at the coffee shop in the hotel. Once they'd ordered, Jodie sipped on her coffee and stared out the window. When she glanced at Dean, he was watching her intently, making her feel more self-conscious than she had before.

Finally she asked, "What are you thinking?"

"I'm concerned that you're already regretting what happened last night."

"It's too late for regrets," she finally replied.

"But you're sorry that it happened."

"It complicates matters."

"In what way?"

She raised her eyebrows. "You know better than I do that this relationship isn't going anywhere."

"I don't know that at all." He sipped his coffee. "Where do you want it to go?"

He'd given her the perfect opening to tell him that she wanted marriage, a home, family and a husband who loved their life. Dean Logan would not want to be that man.

When she didn't answer, he said, "I would never hurt you, you know. What's wrong with us spending our leisure time together? We're both consenting adults. Neither of us has any obligations to someone else."

Thankfully their breakfasts arrived, interrupting the conversation. While they ate, Jodie asked him about the job they'd be doing and what they would do first.

By the time they finished eating, caught a cab and arrived at Steve's office, each of them was concentrating on getting the job done as quickly as possible.

Jodie couldn't help but notice how well they worked together, speaking to each other in a shorthand that they'd developed when she was his secretary. By the end of the day Dean appeared to be pleased with their progress.

"If tomorrow goes as well as today has gone, we'll be ready to fly back to the States day after tomorrow."

"Sounds good," she said. The day had taken its toll on her energy, particularly since she had not gotten much sleep last night. They took a cab back to the hotel. Once there, Jodie said, "I think I'll order in tonight and go to bed as soon as I eat. I'm beat."

"I really worked you today. You did a fine job, by the way."

She clasped her hands in front of her. "If you'll excuse me, I'd like to take a bath before I eat."

He frowned. "Of course. Did I overwork you today?"

"Not really. I guess I used a lot of nervous energy trying to learn so much so quickly."

"You should have said something."

She smiled. "I am."

"I mean sooner."

"I'm fine, Dean. Just very tired."

"I don't feel like eating out either. Tell me what you want to eat and I'll order for us while you take your bath."

She didn't care. She wasn't hungry. She just wanted to have some time alone. "A chef's salad."

When he walked to the phone, she went to her room and closed the door, leaning against it and looking at her bed with longing. It had taken all of her concentration to stay focused on Dean's instructions today instead of thinking about what had happened last night.

She was well and truly hooked on him. The problem was that he had no intention of reeling her in. If she did continue to see him once they returned home, how long would it be before he tossed her back into the water?

Once in the tub, she was soothed by the warm water. She rested her head against the tub and closed her eyes.

Dean glanced at his watch when their meal was delivered. He hadn't heard anything from Jodie in more than half an hour. He tapped on her door. "Jodie? Your salad is here. Are you ready to eat?"

There was no response.

He opened the door and peered inside. The only light was in the bathroom. "Jodie?" He felt a twinge of alarm.

Dean stepped inside and went to the door of her bathroom. When he looked inside, he found her asleep in the tub. A feeling of tenderness washed over him, although he had no idea what the emotion was since he'd rarely felt it.

"Jodie," he said in a firm voice.

Her eyes flew open and she scrambled to sit up.

"Sorry to come in on you but I wanted you to know supper is here." He turned and walked out of the room.

Jodie stared at his retreating back in dismay. He sounded irritable. And then she chuckled. Dean usually sounded irritable, so what was different?

The difference had occurred in his lovemaking last

night, in his murmured endearments, in his eagerness to make love to her as the night passed.

She had definitely provoked him the evening before, therefore she had no one but herself to blame.

Jodie quickly dressed in pajamas and a robe and went into the other room. She found Dean staring out the window, his hands in his pockets. She could see his reflection and he looked grim.

"I'm so sorry for taking so long. As you saw, I fell asleep in the tub."

He turned and walked over to the table that held their food. "I owe you an apology for working you so hard today. I'm used to pushing myself until I get the job done."

"I didn't mind." She sat down at the table. "You should have gone ahead and eaten. Your food must be cold by now."

"Doesn't matter."

They ate in strained silence. Once they were finished, Dean rolled the table into the hall and returned to the sitting room. "I'd like to discuss something with you, if you don't mind."

Her nap had done wonders for her. "Of course," she said and sat on the sofa.

He pulled a chair closer so that he was facing her. "I need to apologize for last night. I had no business coming into your room and getting into the shower with you. Could I plead temporary insanity?"

So that was what had him looking so grim. She smiled. "After what I said to you, how could any red-blooded male have ignored the challenge?"

His shoulders relaxed and he smiled ruefully. "Well, there is that. However, my conscience has gotten the better of me and I need to confess. I brought you along on this trip hoping that something might happen between us."

"I suspected that. You're very aggressive when you set a goal for yourself, and I must have been on your list. Just remember that I was a willing participant last night."

"But you don't like flings."

"That's right. And I don't think we should continue to see each other once we're home. It would be too awkward for both of us. I admire and respect you—" *and love the living daylights out of you* "—but I can't be what you want."

"Exactly what is it I want?"

"A short-term companion who's there when you have time to see her, who can accept what you want without strings attached. Someone like Rachel."

"I thought I made it clear I'm not seeing Rachel—or anyone else, for that matter," he said, sounding frustrated. Dean got up and started pacing. "You make me sound very shallow."

"I don't mean to. Your commitment to the company is total. You have no room for anything but a casual relationship with someone."

"And you're not the casual type, I take it."

"Unfortunately no. However, you never seem to have trouble finding others who will accept the kind of relationship you want."

He stopped pacing and looked at her. "What do you want from me? Am I supposed to declare that my intentions are honorable? That I want to get married and move to the suburbs, have a family and settle into domestic bliss?"

She gazed at him for a long time before she finally said, "I would never suggest such a thing."

"Good. Because I'm definitely not that kind of guy."

"I know," she murmured.

"So last night was an aberration and won't happen again."

"Yes."

He crossed his arms over his chest. "Fine. I can live with that. Is this where I ask if it was as good for you as it was for me?"

She smiled. "It was sensational."

He suddenly sat down again. "Yeah, it was," he said, sounding a little bewildered.

They sat in silence for several minutes before he said, "We'd better get some sleep. Tomorrow's going to be another long day."

Jodie stood and said, "Good night, Dean," and went to her bedroom.

He sat there for a long time, staring blankly out the window. With sudden decision, he left the suite, went downstairs and walked out onto the beach.

He walked the beach until dawn.

Fourteen

Six weeks later

"**M**r. Logan, Mr. Greenfeld is here to see you."

Candace Rudin had taken to her job with alarming ease. She was punctual, efficient, unobtrusive. In all, a well-trained secretary.

Damn, he missed Jodie more and more as each day passed...as a secretary, of course.

"Have Betty send him back, please."

She nodded briskly and went back to her desk.

Candace had quickly learned that he disliked the inter-com and cheerfully came to his office door to give him messages.

Candace was a very nice woman. A little formal, per-haps; she'd told him she wasn't comfortable calling him by his first name. She lived alone except for two cats since her husband died two years ago. Her three children were grown. She didn't mind overtime and put up with his moods.

What more could he want?

While he waited for Greenfeld, Dean stood and walked over to one of his windows.

He hadn't seen Jodie since they'd returned from Hawaii. He'd stopped finding excuses to go to her department to see her. She'd made her position quite clear and he would respect that.

He'd taken dates out to dinner, to see a play or movie and once to a Cubs game. At the end of each evening, though, he'd kissed them good-night at the door and gone home.

None of them stirred him at all, despite their intelligence, their looks and their behavior toward him. The dating scene was really becoming a bore.

He heard Greenfeld greet Candace and turned. "Good to see you, Jacob," he said, walking to the man with his arm outstretched.

"You, too, Dean," Jacob replied with a smile as they shook hands. "Thank you for seeing me."

Dean grinned. "Are you kidding? I was glad to hear from you after all this time. You disappeared after we graduated from college. How've you been?"

Once again Dean immersed himself in business and put all thought of Jodie away…until later that night when he fell asleep hugging his pillow and dreamed he was with her.

What was wrong with him anyway? he asked himself, staring out at the lake the next morning. When had he ever taken no for an answer when he really wanted something?

The truth was, Jodie taking another job in the office had left a big hole in his life—and it wasn't about sex, although that had been great.

He missed seeing her. He missed the sound of her voice. He missed the delicate scent of her perfume. Even if he never made love to her again, he knew he would remember everything about the pleasure of bringing her to a climax, of holding her in his arms afterward.

She'd graduated from college and had not sent him an announcement. He'd sent her a gift anyway and received a polite thank-you note that could have been written to his great-aunt Harriet. If he had a great-aunt Harriet.

He'd hoped that over time she might change her mind and be willing to see him again, but he realized that he'd be tripping over his gray beard before that happened.

It was time for drastic action. As his plan began to appear in his head, he nodded. He was a man of action, after all. Hadn't she mentioned that he was aggressive when he wanted something?

Well, he was ready to admit that he wanted her and no one else.

He would wait no longer to get her back in his life, on whatever terms she set.

"Isn't this a beautiful day," Lynette said, stretched out on a blanket in one of Chicago's parks. "I'm so glad we planned this."

Jodie nodded. She had Emily in her lap and was playing with her while Chuck played catch with the boys.

"Me, too."

"How's it feel to finally be through with school?"

"A little lost, actually. I don't know what to do with all my spare time."

"Well, it's been a boon for me. Chuck and I have certainly enjoyed your staying with the kiddos and giving us some alone time." She grinned. "I feel definitely decadent sleeping until late in the morning once a week."

"You deserve it."

Suddenly Lynette shouted, "Way to go, Kyle, good one." When she turned back to Jodie, she said, "You don't talk about work much anymore. Why is that?"

Jodie shrugged. "Nothing to talk about. I'm learning so much stuff that my head spins at times, but I'm enjoying it."

"And we're still not going to discuss Dean, are we?"

"There's nothing to discuss. I haven't seen…" Her voice trailed off.

"What's wrong?"

"If I'm not mistaken, that's Dean Logan coming toward us now."

Lynette sat up. "Really? Where?"

Jodie nodded toward the man drawing closer.

"You're kidding me," Lynette said in awe. "He's gorgeous. And you always said he looked like he should be on Mount Rushmore with his great stone face."

"He could."

"The grin he's wearing could melt rock, honey. And I believe it's directed at you!"

"Hi," he said when he reached them. "I thought that was you." He glanced at Lynette and back at Jodie. "Mind if I join you?"

Before Jodie could find her tongue, Lynette scooted over

and patted the blanket. "We'd be delighted. Wouldn't we, Jodie?" she asked, her eyes wide in mocking innocence.

He didn't wait for her answer but sat on the blanket.

"What are you doing—" Jodie began to ask when the boys interrupted her.

"Hi!" Kyle said. "Do you know our aunt Jodie? We have sleepovers at her house and she's—"

"Hush!" Lynette said, gaining Jodie's eternal gratitude for stopping him. Kyle wasn't known for his tact or diplomacy.

"Dean, I'd like you to meet my sister, Lynette, and her children." She nodded to the boys. "Kent and Kyle." Then she looked down to the infant in her arms and said, "This is Emily."

Chuck joined them. "Hi. Chuck Patterson," he said, his hand out.

Dean shook hands. "Dean Logan."

"Ah," was all Chuck said.

"I don't care what rumors Jodie has brought home to you, it isn't true that I eat young children for breakfast."

"Ooooh, gross!" Kent said with a grin.

Chuck sat down. "Why don't you let me rest for a few minutes, guys? Go toss the ball between you."

When the two of them moved away, he turned and looked at Lynette in disbelief. "Did you see that? They actually minded me. And without argument." He looked at Jodie. "Boy, if you ever decide to hire yourself out as a nanny, I can give you a glowing recommendation."

"If you haven't already guessed, Chuck is my brother-in-law."

Chuck reached for the ice chest. "Would you like something to drink? We have colas, lemonade and water."

"Water sounds great," Dean said.

Chuck pulled out two bottles of water. He gave one to Dean and rolled the other across his forehead. "I'm getting too old for this," he said, grinning.

Jodie cleared her throat. "What a coincidence that you should be at the same park we chose."

Dean smiled blandly. "Isn't it?" He turned and asked Chuck about his police work, giving her no chance to probe any further.

When they were packing things to go home, Lynette suddenly said, "Dean, why don't you come have supper with us tonight? You and Chuck seem to have a lot to discuss."

"Oh, I'm sure he's—" Jodie leaped in to the conversation just as Dean replied.

"That sounds great, Lynette. Thanks."

"—too busy," Jodie ended lamely.

"Don't expect anything fancy. It will probably be leftovers."

"My favorite meal."

Chuck and Lynette laughed.

Jodie glanced away for a moment before she said, "Look, you guys, why don't you go on and I'll get home. I have a dozen things to do and—"

Lynette gave her the famous big-sister stare for a moment before she replied, "Nonsense. We'll meet you over there."

Jodie watched them head to their car in silence.

"If you don't want me to go, I can make my excuses," Dean said quietly.

She shook her head, unable to say anything.

"What's wrong with my getting to know your family?"

"Nothing at all. Why do you want to?"

"Because I've missed you. I thought we were friends. We worked amicably together for several years. Now I feel like a leper where you're concerned."

She took a deep breath. "It's called self-preservation, Dean. I thought we'd come to an understanding. I don't want to get hurt."

"I would never hurt you."

"Not intentionally, I'm sure."

"Let's make a deal. Let's spend the next three months seeing each other as friends. Strictly platonic. I'd like to spend time with you, that's all."

"Friends. You think we can do that?"

He grinned. "I can if you can."

She sighed and then held out her hand. "Well, friend, we'd better get over to Lynette's before she sends Chuck out to find us. I wouldn't put it past him to put out an all points bulletin over the police scanner if we don't get a move on."

Fifteen

"Lighten up, sis, would you, please? I've never seen you so quiet!"

Jodie picked up a large salad and a platter of spaghetti and headed to the dining area. "I thought you'd appreciate the fact that I'm not talking your ear off!"

Lynette followed her with a large bowl of sauce that'd she'd removed from the freezer and heated, together with a basket of French bread drenched in garlic butter.

Jodie could hear Dean and Chuck chatting away in the living room like old buddies.

The sisters paused and looked at the table to be sure everything was ready. Lynette glanced at Jodie. "You've been keeping secrets, haven't you, sis?"

Jodie's heart lurched. "What do you mean?"

"That man is more than a boss to you. The way he looks at you is a dead giveaway."

"Oh, please. We've known each other for several years. We had a comfortable relationship when I worked for him. I rarely see him now."

"Whatever you say, dear," Lynette replied. She walked into the living room and said, "Sorry to interrupt your bonding, guys, but dinner, such as it is, is served."

"Lynette!" Jodie snapped from behind her.

Lynette turned and said, "I repeat. Lighten up."

Within five minutes Dean had charmed the Patterson family. His behavior contradicted everything she'd ever told them about him. Great. Now she looked like a liar.

Dean interrupted her glum thoughts by saying, "Jodie, why don't we catch a movie tomorrow and maybe have dinner afterward?"

Before she could respond, Kent piped up with, "She's your girlfriend, isn't she, Mr. Logan?"

Okay. That was it. Jodie saw no hope for her except to silently slide out of her chair and under the table.

"Well, Kent," Dean replied, winning points for remembering his name, "we are definitely friends—very good friends."

Kyle went into action. "Are you going to marry her?"

Jodie knew her face flushed a fiery red while Chuck scolded the boys. "It's not polite to ask personal questions, boys," Chuck said sternly. "Now eat your dinner."

When Jodie glanced at Dean, he winked at her, causing her to shake her head and shrug.

Thankfully Chuck introduced an innocuous subject that lasted through the rest of the meal.

Once dinner was over, Jodie helped Lynette clear the

table and load the dishwasher. She'd wiped down the counters when Emily cried out.

Lynette looked at her watch. "Right on time. I'd better go feed her."

"And I need to get home. Thanks for dinner again. Two nights in a row seems a little excessive."

"Don't worry about it. You know you're welcome anytime."

Lynette went upstairs and Jodie returned to the living room. "I'm going home now. Thanks for everything," she said to Chuck.

Dean immediately stood. "I need to go, as well." He turned to Chuck. "Enjoyed getting to know you. We'll have to find the time to go to a Cubs game soon."

Chuck also stood. "Sounds like a plan, Dean." He hugged Jodie. "Take care, sweetheart."

Jodie and Dean went outside to where they had parked their cars. She turned to say something when she realized he was right behind her.

"You never answered my question," he said, his hand massaging the nape of her neck.

She took a deep breath before saying, "Thank you for asking, and yes, I'd enjoy going to the movie with you." There. She'd just dived into the deep end.

He grinned. "See how easy that was?" He leaned closer and kissed her, his hand still caressing her neck and shoulders. As usual, the casual kiss turned into much more, and when they stepped away from each other, her heart was pounding so hard she wondered if she was having a heart attack or a stroke.

"That was a little more than a friendly kiss," she managed to say, catching her breath.

He shrugged. "What can I say? All's fair in love and war."

"Which one are we talking about?" she asked.

He gave her a brief hug and turned. "You'll have to figure that one out on your own," he said over his shoulder as he strode to his car.

When Jodie got home that night, she faced her fears. Of course, he hadn't been serious about being in love with her. He'd been up-front about what he wanted from her. Friendship. There was no reason in the world to run away from a friendship. The only way she could get hurt was to hope for some kind of commitment from Dean, which she knew she'd never get. One of the reasons his relationships ended was because the women wanted to marry him. She knew because she'd listened to a few who'd hoped she would put in a good word with him.

Lynette was absolutely right. She needed to lighten up. It wouldn't be the end of her world when he moved on to someone else. She wouldn't let it be.

She spent the next hour trying to figure out what to wear tomorrow.

Once home, Dean wondered why he'd mentioned love or war. Seeing Jodie was neither love nor war. He missed her, that's all. He'd always enjoyed being around her. What was wrong with that?

She'd made it clear she would not go to bed with him. He'd accept that. He didn't particularly like it, but he'd accept it in exchange for having her in his life again.

Dean looked at the stack of papers he'd brought home earlier today. When was he going to have time to go over them? Not tonight, anyway. He'd review them in the morning before he left to pick up Jodie. He'd never let his social life interfere with business before, but what he didn't get done, he'd do at the office on Monday.

He'd enjoyed seeing her again and meeting some of her family. He and Chuck had clicked. Chuck had been friendly without being overbearing, and Jodie's name had never been mentioned between them.

Once in bed, he thought about Jodie until he fell asleep.

"I can't remember laughing so hard in a long time," Jodie told Dean once they left the movie theater the next evening. "My sides hurt."

"I can relate," he replied with a smile. "I'm glad you enjoyed it."

She had, and not just the movie. They'd watched the comedy with fingers entwined like a couple of teenagers. Dean had laughed out loud on a few occasions, and the sound had cheered her. Maybe she did have an influence on him, since she couldn't imagine his going alone to see a movie.

Once seated in a Greek restaurant, they ordered. Over their salads Jodie asked, "Everything still working out with Mrs. Rudin?"

"She's very efficient. What I hadn't realized was how often you and I discussed business matters. You were my sounding board for most of my decisions. I hadn't realized it until after you were gone."

"If I can help, you know I'd be happy to."

"Thank you. I also have a request to make…more like a plea, actually." He looked grim. "There's a dinner and dance I'm expected to attend on Saturday night. I'd skip attending it since I've already made my donation, except that I'm one of the speakers. It's a benefit to raise money for Alzheimer's." He paused a moment. "My mother was diagnosed with the disease a while ago, so if they need me to make a speech, I will. I just hate like hell to go by myself and I'm not seeing anyone these days."

"Of course I'll go with you, Dean. I'd like to hear you speak."

"No, you wouldn't, believe me. The regularly scheduled speaker was forced to cancel at the last minute, so I'm filling in for him."

Dean still wasn't seeing anyone? How strange. Dean was never one to wait to find someone else when one of his relationships faltered. Of course, they'd never had a relationship—except for work…and when they'd visited Hawaii. But other than that, she hadn't seen or heard from him. He was a virile male who never lacked having a woman in his bed.

However, it was none of her business and she didn't comment on that part of his remarks.

They discussed several business matters during their meal, falling into a familiar routine. Jodie felt comfortable with Dean for the first time since she'd gone to Hawaii with him—that is, until they reached her front door.

She turned to him and said a little stiffly, "Thank you for this evening."

He lifted an eyebrow. "Aren't you going to invite me inside?"

"No."

"Even if I beg?"

She chuckled. "Dean, if I invite you inside, we both know that we'll probably end up in bed together."

"And your point is?"

"That's a little too friendly for me, I'm afraid."

"Okay."

She looked at him quizzically. "Okay?"

He shrugged. "You're right, that's all. Our relationship is strictly platonic, I swear." He held up his right hand. After a moment he asked, "Is it all right if I kiss you good night?"

She glanced down the deserted hallway and felt that her self-restraint would be helped by being there. "Okay."

He took his time pulling her closer to him. He started by nibbling on her earlobe before he planted small kisses along her jawline. Just as she knew it would, Jodie felt her control slipping. She moved her hands from his chest to around his neck, and when he finally found her mouth she was more than ready for him.

The kiss went on and on until the sound of the elevator brought her back to reality. She released him, gasping a little. Her body quivered with passion, which he knew darned well.

His smile was slow and intimate.

A couple got off the elevator and turned the other way without seeing them.

"Good night," Dean said gently. "Pleasant dreams." He turned and walked to the elevator, which conveniently opened when he pushed the button. She stepped in quickly, watching Dean until the door closed.

Jodie closed and locked the door and made it to her bedroom on wobbly knees before collapsing on the bed.

Who had she been kidding? Whether she saw Dean or not, her emotions were in a tangle where he was concerned.

Of course she wanted to experience again what they'd shared in that Honolulu hotel. He aroused a passion in her she'd never known existed. Now he was using that knowledge to remind her what they could have if she wanted an intimate relationship with him.

However, she was determined not to give in to her baser instincts. She would not. She could not.

Which meant that another restless night awaited her.

Sixteen

Jodie opened her door on Saturday evening to find Dean Logan looking drop-dead gorgeous in a tuxedo that was obviously custom made. His shoulders looked broader than ever, and since she vividly recalled how they felt beneath her fingers, she found it difficult to speak.

She finally said, "Come in," sounding hoarse. She cleared her throat.

He paused in the doorway for a moment before stepping inside. "I'm early. I apologize."

"No apology needed." She picked up her evening bag and tried not to notice the way he looked at her. During another shopping trip she'd found what she considered to be the perfect little black dress to wear. The style was deceptively simple and she knew she looked good wearing it.

Dean's look made clear that he approved and it made clear that he wanted her.

Some friendship this is going to be. Who was she kidding anyway?

So why are you willing to see him?

Because I have a masochistic streak in me, that's why.

Oh.

She picked up a lacy stole and slipped it around her shoulders.

They were silent in the elevator. Once in the car, Dean turned to her and said, "Is it overstepping the boundaries of friendship to say you are a knockout in that dress?"

She smiled demurely. "Thank you." He started the car after a quick shake of his head, as though clearing his brain. "Have you decided what you plan to say tonight?" she asked.

Once on the street, he replied, "I suppose. I never say what I've written anyway. All I know is that it will be short."

They pulled into one of the large conference centers and turned the car over to the valet. Other people in formal dress converged on the entrance to the hotel, and Dean guided her along in the same direction.

Several people spoke to him while eyeing her surreptitiously. He introduced her briefly to those who stopped to speak to him.

They'd almost reached the ballroom when Jodie heard a familiar voice behind them.

"Dean! I thought that was you. I never expected to see you at one of these things."

They stopped and Dean turned. "Hello, Rachel." He

recognized her escort. "Good to see you, Bailey," Dean said and shook his hand.

In a bright voice Rachel began to say, "So aren't you going to introduce us to—"

At that point, Jodie reluctantly turned to face them.

"Jodie? Is that really you? You look— I mean, uh, it's good to see you again." The look she gave both of them belied the comment. "So," she said to Dean, "I'm surprised to see you with your secretary." Her implication that he'd resorted to attending the gathering with the hired help wasn't lost on either of them.

"Actually," Dean said, looking amused, "she no longer works for me. She's working in Engineering now."

Jodie looked down at her toes. She could imagine Rachel's guess at how she got the promotion. She mentally squared her shoulders and looked Rachel in the eye. "That's true. I graduated from school at long last. Dean told me a few years ago that when I got my degree he'd move me into one of the other departments."

Rachel looked at Dean. "I bet you're lost without her…being your secretary."

"Somehow I've managed to survive," he replied wryly.

Once the two couples entered the ballroom, Rachel looked around and said to Bailey, "Do you recall our table number?" and they drifted away from Dean and Jodie.

Jodie looked up at him. "Rachel's looking good, don't you think?"

He frowned slightly. "I guess she looked okay. I didn't notice." He started toward the front of the room where the dais was set up. "We're at table one."

When they drew closer, Jodie saw that their table was

filled except for the two seats reserved for them. She recognized a couple of the men but only because she'd seen their photographs in the paper.

The movers and shakers of Chicago were there tonight. Dean hadn't told her that the affair would be so well attended. She wondered if the size of the crowd would bother Dean. She'd never thought of him being a public speaker.

Dean introduced her to the table at large. Everyone was gracious and she found herself relaxing—until one of the wives asked, "What branch of the Cameron family are you, my dear?"

"The Wisconsin branch."

"Oh." The woman sounded disappointed. "You're not related to any of the Camerons here in Chicago?"

Jodie smiled politely, wishing for the evening to end. Right now. "Not that I'm aware of."

"Pity. I suppose you've traced your roots back to Scotland."

"Not yet."

"Genealogy is fascinating work. You'll enjoy it once you get started."

Jodie was relieved when the waiters came out with their salads and the conversation became more general.

She hated feeling so inadequate in situations such as this. She thought about telling the woman that her mother was a waitress in Phoenix just to see her reaction.

As the meal progressed, Jodie was surprised to discover that the food was delicious. No telling how much the meal had cost, but it was a vast improvement on the rubber chicken usually served at the events she'd attended.

After dinner the emcee of the event spoke to the gathering, thanking them for coming and introducing Dean as the speaker.

Why she should feel so nervous for him she had no idea, because he appeared composed enough as he strode to the dais.

Within minutes after he started speaking he had the room mesmerized. He drew from his personal experience and the pain involved watching a loved one slip away from reality.

As promised, he kept his speech short and very much to the point and when he finished, he received a standing ovation. Jodie stood with the rest, tears in her eyes. She'd never been more proud of him.

The emcee thanked him and told everyone to enjoy the music and dancing. The dance floor filled quickly with the first song. Everyone at their table was on the dance floor when Dean turned to her. "Shall we dance?"

Jodie nodded and they walked out onto the floor. Once they were dancing, she said, "I was impressed with your speech. Your calm discussion of such a personal and painful situation touched us all."

"I felt it was the best way to explain the need for more money for research."

"You are a man of many talents, Mr. Logan."

He pulled her closer to him and she put her head on his chest. She was surprised to discover his heart racing and lifted her head.

"Sorry. I react this way when I'm around you."

Only then did she realize that he was aroused. She couldn't help blushing.

"Would you prefer not to dance?" he finally asked.

"Oh, Dean, you're making things very difficult for me."

"And you have a way of making things hard for me."

"It's not that I'm playing hard to get…."

"I know. It's not your fault that I can't stop myself from reacting to you." He continued to dance but held her a few inches away from him. "This friendship thing isn't working."

She shook her head, unable to speak. That's when she knew what she had to do. "All right then."

"All right what?"

"I'll sleep with you tonight."

He stopped dead in his tracks, causing another couple to run into them. "Sorry," he said and slipped his arm around Jodie's waist. "Please tell me that you're serious," he said roughly.

She nodded, her gaze direct. "I'm serious."

"We need to go," he said. He took her hand and started off the dance floor before the song finished.

Jodie remained silent while they waited for his car to be brought around, and neither of them spoke on the way to her apartment. She realized that she quivered with need, a need she'd tried to ignore for weeks. She wanted him. She wanted him now.

The door barely closed behind them when he lifted her, pulling her legs around his waist, leaned her against the door, fumbled with his zipper and shoved inside her as he ripped her panties.

Their lovemaking was hot, strong and very passionate, both of them climaxing within minutes. Dean gathered her closer and walked—as much as he was able to with his pants around his ankles—into her bedroom, where he carefully placed her on the bed.

She watched him remove his tuxedo and allowed him to slip her dress and underthings off her. Still without speaking, he joined her on the bed and made slow, sensuous love to her. They responded to each other as they had in Hawaii. Jodie knew that she would never, ever, forget this night.

He left at dawn.

The following Monday morning Jodie handed Frank her resignation. By that afternoon, she was on the road heading south.

Seventeen

Dean called Jodie's apartment several times on Sunday but got no answer. He figured she'd gone to her sister's and he fought the temptation to call her there just to hear her voice.

He owed her an apology for his Neanderthal behavior Saturday night. The problem was, he couldn't promise that he wouldn't behave the same way the next time they were alone.

What kind of spell was he under that she was on his mind most of the time? All right, all of the time. He'd be in meetings with clients and his mind would wander.

This was not the way he'd ever conducted himself and he didn't like it. The problem was that he didn't know what to do about it.

On Monday he had back-to-back meetings, most of them out of the office, and he didn't return until after four.

He decided to check with Jodie to see if she'd like to have dinner with him that night. Nothing wrong with that. He'd make certain they weren't alone, either during their meal or when he took her home. He would show her that he could, in fact, restrain himself around her, but being alone with her would be too much for him.

For that matter, he could bring her back to the office to get her car.

Feeling pleased with his plan, Dean went to the department where she worked. When he didn't see her, he strolled into Frank's office.

Frank looked up. "How did the meeting with Flynn go today?"

"He liked the presentation you made last week and he's ready to sign on."

"Good to hear."

"I, uh, was looking for Jodie. Did she go home early?"

Frank frowned. "Didn't she tell you?"

"Tell me what?"

"She resigned this morning—used her vacation time in lieu of notice and left."

Dean sank into the nearest chair. He felt as though Frank had punched him in the diaphragm, knocking the breath out of him. When he didn't say anything, Frank said, "I figured you knew about it."

"No. No, I didn't." He was quiet for a moment and then asked, "Did she say why. I thought she was happy here. Did she mention another job?"

"Sorry. Actually she said very little, just cleaned out her desk. I'll admit, I hated to see her go. She's good. Sharp. Creative. In the time she's worked for me, I've been very impressed with her work. She was one of the people who worked on the presentation I made."

Dean nodded, although he didn't hear what Frank had said. His mind was racing with questions. Why had she quit so abruptly? And without telling him?

What the hell was going on?

"You all right?" Frank asked after a lengthy silence.

"I'm fine. Just surprised. The news caught me off guard, that's all." He stood up and said, "I'll talk to you later."

Dean didn't go to his office to check messages or mail. He went directly to the parking garage, got into his car and drove to Jodie's apartment.

There was no answer after repeated knocks.

His next stop was the Pattersons' home. As soon as he knocked, the door opened wide. It was Kent.

"Hi," Kent said with a big smile.

Dean returned his smile. "Hello, Kent. Is your mom home?"

"Uh-huh." He turned away and yelled, "Mom, it's Aunt Jodie's boyfriend."

"Have him come in and have a seat. I'll be there shortly."

Dean stepped inside. A tornado had recently come through the living room, judging from the scattered toys, shoes and jackets.

"Can I get you something to drink?" Kent asked politely.

"No, thank you."

"Oh." Kent sat across from Dean and looked at a loss as to what to do next.

"Don't let me interrupt whatever you were doing," Dean said, equally polite.

Kent grinned. "Okay," he replied and immediately slid

to the floor, where he'd been playing with small racing cars on a track that wound around the couch.

Lynette came hurrying in a few minutes later. "I'm so sorry to keep you waiting. I just got home from picking up the boys at school and it was time to feed Emily."

"No problem."

Lynette immediately began picking up toys, coats and shoes. "I'd apologize for the way the house looks except it would be a waste of time, since this is the way it looks more often than not."

"I won't keep you. I dropped by to see if you've talked to Jodie in the last day or two."

Lynette straightened and looked at him, obviously puzzled. She sat down in the chair recently vacated by her son. "She was here Friday night."

"Did you talk to her yesterday or today?"

"No. What's wrong? Has something happened to her?" she asked, making no effort to hide her alarm.

"That's what I'm trying to find out. She quit her job today, used accrued vacation time as her notice and left."

Lynette placed her hand on the side of her neck. "Good heavens. I had no idea she was considering such a thing."

"Neither did I. We went out Saturday night and she seemed to be fine when I left. I thought you might have some idea why she quit and where she might be."

She shook her head. "I'm sorry, but I don't. Have you tried her apartment?"

He nodded. "And I've left several messages on her machine."

"I'll call Chuck and have him check out her apartment. I hope nothing's happened to her."

She picked up the phone and made the call. When Chuck answered his cell phone, she told him what she'd just learned. After she hung up, she said, "He'll go check. Do you want to wait here for him to call back?"

He stood. "That won't be necessary. I'd appreciate your calling me when you find out anything." He gave her his cell phone number and left.

His phone rang as he parked his car at his condominium. "Logan."

"Hi, Dean, this is Lynette. Things are getting more and more curious. Chuck said her apartment looks okay but most of her clothes and personal things are gone."

Numbly he replied, "Thanks for letting me know."

"No problem. I'm sure I'll hear from her soon. She isn't one to want people to worry about her, which is why all this is such a surprise. This isn't like Jodie at all. Anyway, I'll have her call you when I hear from her."

"Thank you."

He pocketed the phone and walked to the elevator.

Was it something he'd said Saturday night? Or done? Or did her disappearance have nothing to do with him?

He had no way of knowing.

Friday morning Lynette's phone rang. When she answered, Jodie said, "Hi, sis. Thought I'd let you know I won't be there for dinner tonight."

"Joanna Louise Cameron, where in the world are you? I've been frantic since Monday when Dean told me you'd quit your job."

"Dean told you?"

"Yes. When he couldn't reach you at home, he came

over here to see if I knew anything. Chuck went to your apartment to see if you had been hurt or worse. Why didn't you let anyone know where you were going?"

"Because I wasn't sure where I intended to go when I left Chicago."

"Where are you?"

"I showed up here at Mom's late last night. I plan to stay a while and will probably look for a job down here."

"Have you lost your ever lovin' mind? What's wrong with the job you had here? You loved it. You were excited about it."

Lynette heard Jodie sigh. Finally she said, "It's a long story."

"I've got time to hear a long story. The boys are in school and Emily just went down for her nap. Tell me."

Jodie wasn't ready to talk about Dean to anyone, but she knew she owed Lynette an explanation. Finally she said, "I had to get away from Dean."

Silence greeted her admission. Finally in a horrified voice Lynette asked, "What did he do? It must have been serious for you to run like this. Did you call the police?"

"It's nothing like that, Lynette. I did a really stupid thing and it's so trite I'm embarrassed to admit it. I fell in love with my boss."

"So? He appears deeply enamored of you, as well."

"Not really. He decided he wanted for us to date and I agreed. I truly thought I could handle my response to him, but I can't. Whenever he's nearby, all he has to do is look at me and I go up in flames."

"Oh, honey. There's absolutely nothing wrong with that. Is that what scared you away?"

"Partly. The thing about Dean—and he's the first to admit it—is he isn't interested in a long-term commitment. And that's the only kind I want. I've been careful not to tell him how I feel, but now he's going to guess that I'm crazy about him. Once a woman tells him she's in love with him, he practically leaves skid marks getting away from her.

"So I decided that it would be better for me to leave before I had to go through that. I've tried to make a clean break with him, but somehow I end up going out with him again. I have no willpower where he's concerned. None. So I realized that I would have to go someplace where there was no chance of running into him. So I resigned."

"Maybe you're different. Maybe he'd be willing—"

"No. It's our ego that tells us that we can cause a person to change if we just love them enough. That's our fantasy, but the reality is that Dean knows what he wants and has no reason to change."

"Maybe so," Lynette replied. "But he was very concerned about you. I told him I'd have you call him. I guess that's not going to happen."

Jodie rubbed her forehead where a headache loomed. "I'll admit, I didn't expect him to contact you. If you should hear from him again—which I very much doubt—tell him whatever you want, but don't tell him that I'm in love with him. I want that to be our little secret, Lynette, okay?"

"I don't keep secrets from Chuck."

"All right. Tell Chuck. That's all."

"Well, honey, you have to do what you have to do, I suppose. I can't bear the idea of you living so far away. How's Mom taking all this?"

"I haven't told her. She had to leave early to go to work at the diner. She'll be home a little after two."

"Maybe you can convince her she doesn't have to work. Each of us is contributing to her support. It's not as though she has to work."

"She knows that, but she said she'd miss visiting with the locals who stop in every day. You know Mom. She loves people. I'm sure she's in her element there."

"Try to get some rest. That's a long trip from here."

"Tell me about it. I'm going back to bed. I'll talk to you later."

Lynette hung up the phone and immediately called Chuck. As soon as he answered, she told him about the call.

"So she ran away," Chuck summed up.

"Yes."

"That's too bad."

"I promised her that I wouldn't tell anyone but you about her feelings for Dean."

"Okay."

"However…you didn't make her any promises. So if you wanted to let Dean know…"

"No way am I going to get involved in any matchmaking. I don't need both of them cursing me. Come on, sweetheart; let her live her life the way she wants."

"Even if she's miserable?"

"Yes."

"Oh, Chuck, why do you have to be such a guy!"

"What? What, may I ask, is wrong with being a guy?"

"You just don't understand women."

"Probably. Especially at the moment. I haven't a clue what you're upset about."

"I'm upset because you have the opportunity to get two people who love each other together. That's not matchmaking. They've made the connection. They're obviously involved with each other. At least give Dean the information, okay? Then whatever he does about it will be up to him."

After a moment of silence Chuck grudgingly replied, "I'll think about it."

"You do that and I'll be eternally grateful—and I will express my gratitude in a number of creative ways."

Eighteen

Candace stepped to Dean's door a few days later and said, "There's a Mr. Chuck Patterson on line two. Shall I get his number and have you call him back?"

Without answering her question, Dean grabbed the phone. "Chuck! Good to hear from you. Hold on a minute, will you?" He raised his voice slightly and said, "Candace, please close the door and hold my calls."

He uncovered the mouthpiece of the phone and asked, "Have you heard from her?"

There was a pause and then Dean heard Chuck's laugh. "You've got it bad, my friend. I called to see if you wanted to go to the Cubs game tomorrow afternoon. My treat."

"Oh. Let me check my schedule." He looked at his calendar. He had two appointments that morning but none in the afternoon. "Sounds good. Where should I meet you?"

"I'll pick you up in front of your building," Chuck replied and named a time.

"Okay. Is she all right?" Dean asked.

"She's fine, Dean. She's visiting her mother. We can talk more tomorrow."

"See you then," Dean said and hung up the phone.

She was in Phoenix? Just like that, she quits her job, walks out on him without a word and goes to see her mother?

It would seem so.

Dean and Chuck arrived at the game early. They'd talked about everything under the sun on the ride to the stadium... everything but Jodie's sudden departure.

At any other time Dean would have enjoyed Chuck's company, but knowing that he was withholding information about Jodie made Dean want to throttle him.

At long last Chuck brought up the subject by throwing Dean a curveball. "So what's going on between you and Jodie anyway?"

"Uh, well, I mean, we've known each other quite a while. She was my secretary for several years."

"I understand that and that's not what I'm talking about. Most men don't respond to a former secretary leaving as you have."

Dean nodded. Chuck wasn't going to accept any vague remarks. If he wanted to know what was going on with Jodie, he'd have to bare his soul. Since he was a very private man, he found the idea excruciatingly painful...almost as painful as missing Jodie.

"I finally faced the fact that I'm in love with her, that

I've probably been in love with her for years and was too dumb to recognize it. I've done some really stupid things in my life, but letting her slip away from me like this has to be the biggest mistake I've ever made."

The sentence hung in the air and seemed to expand on the breeze. There. He'd said it. Too bad he hadn't realized that what he felt for her was love until after she was gone.

"That right?" Chuck asked with a smile.

"Yeah."

"So her leaving like that has been tough on you."

"You could say that." What an understatement that was.

"What did she say when you told her?"

"What? That I love her?"

"I believe that's the topic of this conversation, yes."

"I never told her," Dean mumbled.

"Sorry, I didn't catch that."

Dean cleared his throat. "I said that I never told her, fool that I am, because I didn't realize it until very recently."

"I see."

"So how is she? Have you talked with her? Do you know when she plans to come back?"

"I haven't talked with her, but Lynette said she seems to be doing okay. Jodie told her that she might look for a job in Phoenix."

"What! You're kidding, right?"

"Nope. That's what Lynette reported to me."

The crowd roared its approval about something. Chuck and Dean hadn't been paying attention when the game started, and the Cubs were up to bat.

"Looks like a single," Chuck commented.

"Yeah."

"I don't know if you want to hear any suggestions from me," Chuck said briskly, "but here's one anyway—go to Arizona and tell her how you feel. I'm sure the news would have more impact with her if you're there in person."

"I could do that."

"Good. Now, then. Let's watch the game, okay?"

Jodie had been at her mother's for two weeks and was getting restless. She missed work. She'd been tempted to call Frank to see how things were going until she remembered that she no longer had a job.

She'd set up a couple of job interviews for the following week, but in the meantime there was nothing much for her to do. The house was spotless and her mom's garden had already been weeded within an inch of its life.

This morning she decided to enjoy the early-morning coolness outdoors before the sun got too hot.

She loved her mom's backyard. It was very private, with a six-foot wall surrounding it. Inside the wall her mom had planted all kinds of colorful flowering plants, which reminded Jodie of the lush foliage in Hawaii.

Jodie put on a two-piece bathing suit and, once outside, stretched out on one of the lounge chairs and removed the top to her swimsuit. A small hand towel covered her breasts, leaving her shoulders bare. Next she picked up the book she had started the night before and began to read.

Sometime later the doorbell startled her awake, and she realized that she'd dozed off. She considered getting up and answering the door, but she was too relaxed to move. Besides, all of her mom's friends knew that she worked mornings. It was probably some kind of salesman.

She decided to ignore the door and let her eyes close, basking in the quiet and serenity. She'd had trouble sleeping since she'd been there, and from her reflection in the mirror each morning she knew the lack of sleep had taken its toll on her.

"Ah, there you are."

Jodie's immediate reaction to the sound of a very familiar voice was to scream involuntarily and jerk upright.

"Sorry. Didn't mean to startle you," Dean said. "When no one answered the door, I decided to check back here." He looked around. "The garden is beautiful by the way."

When she could speak, she said, "What are you doing here!" Without waiting for an answer, she grabbed a large towel and wrapped it around her.

"Mind if I sit down?" he asked, his voice bland.

She stared at him as though he were an apparition. Finally she nodded.

Once he sat down, he took his time looking her over, from her ponytail to her freshly painted toenails.

"You're looking rested," he said, which she knew to be a lie. He wore a golf shirt and slacks, the shirt clinging to his wide chest and his pants outlining his massive thighs.

"Did you ever play football?" she blurted out. How did that manage to pop out of her mouth? She was losing it.

The look on his face was indescribable. He finally answered, "Yes, in high school and college. Why do you ask?"

"Just curious," she replied faintly. "If you'll excuse me, I'll, uh, go get us something to drink." She didn't give him time to respond before she fled the patio, ignoring the kitchen and racing down the hallway to her room.

She quickly put on some clothes.

Dean Logan was there? In Phoenix? This couldn't be happening. What was she going to have to do, find some deserted island somewhere to make certain she didn't see him?

She hurried into the kitchen, removed a pitcher of lemonade from the fridge and set it on a tray. She added two glasses filled with ice and returned outside.

Dean watched her walk toward him without expression. She placed the tray on the table between them and poured the juice. Once seated, she glanced quickly at him, then away.

She took a swallow of lemonade to aid her dry mouth. "You haven't answered my question. What are you doing here?"

He leaned back in his chair and looked around the garden. "The same thing you are. Enjoying the sun."

"How did you know where I was?"

He lifted his brow. "Was it supposed to be a secret?"

She shrugged. Lynette probably told him. Jodie hadn't told her not to mention her whereabouts to him for the simple reason that she hadn't expected him to come looking for her.

When she didn't comment, he said, "I decided that I work much too hard. I work ridiculously long hours and have a slave driver for a boss." He paused and drank some lemonade. "I decided to follow your example. I quit my job and came to Arizona."

"What do you mean you quit your job? That's impossible."

"Actually it isn't, because I did it. Others can manage the place as well as I can. I've trained them well."

"You could barely get through a week away from the office when we were in Hawaii the first time. The only way you managed was to call the office several times a day."

"Once I realized that I am, in fact, a workaholic, I decided it was time to change my lifestyle."

"So you came to Phoenix? This isn't the best time of year to visit, unless you're looking for sunstroke. I never stay out later than ten o'clock for that reason."

What was the matter with her? She was babbling. The last thing she would have expected was for him to come there.

He sipped from his glass, looking totally relaxed. "Actually Chuck happened to mention that you were visiting your mother while we were at a Cubs game together." He gave her a steady look. "You left without telling me you were leaving, and I thought I'd find out what I had done to offend you."

This was exactly why she'd left Chicago—to avoid explaining why she couldn't deal with their relationship. "You didn't do a thing, Dean," she finally said.

As though she hadn't spoken, he said, "I've been thinking about our last night together. You gave no hint that you intended to walk away from your career and leave town. May I ask why?"

"It was a personal decision I made. I didn't tell anyone."

"I got quite a shock learning that you'd resigned. You seemed to be enjoying your new position."

"Dean, I really don't want to discuss this."

"The thing is, I feel like a fool," he went on to say. "I've been pretending that it didn't matter to me whether I saw you or not, when the truth is I want to be with you all the time." He paused and scrubbed his hand over his face. "I'm not saying this right. What I'm trying to say is that what we have together is too precious to let go of. I want to share my future with you. I thought if I came here and told you that I finally figured out that I'm crazy in love with you—and have been for who knows how long—that you might consider marrying me."

All right. Now she knew she was hallucinating. Dean Logan proposing marriage? It was almost laughable…if she felt in the least like laughing. Which she didn't.

"How quickly we forget," she said. "It was only a couple of months ago when you told me that a commitment and marriage were the very last things you were interested in." She glared at him. "Remember? No house in the suburbs for you. No tiny people to make claims on your time."

She was proud of her little speech. Too bad her teeth were chattering with nerves during the whole thing.

"That was a dying man going under for the third time, unaware that it was way too late for him to be spouting such nonsense."

"Nonsense?"

He leaned toward her and took her hand, which lay limply on her thigh. "It must already be in the nineties out here and you're chilled." He stood and started toward the sliding glass doors into the house. "I'll find something to wrap around you."

She jumped to her feet and followed him into the house. He didn't pause but continued down the hallway looking into rooms. He saw a crocheted afghan lying on the foot of her mother's bed, swept it up and returned to the hall, where he wrapped it around her. Then he pulled her close, holding her tightly against him.

"I know I've given you every reason to believe that I'm a confirmed bachelor. My only excuse is that I'd convinced myself, as well. My feelings for you have always been there, but it wasn't until we went to Hawaii the first time that they shot to the surface. I just didn't recognize them for what they were at the time."

She pulled away from him and walked to the living room, where she sank into her mom's cushy chair. "I'm sorry, but I'm having a little trouble taking all of this in," she said, feeling light-headed. She must have gotten too much sun.

He knelt beside her chair. "I want what Chuck and Lynette have—a lovely home, three great kids and, yes, a place in the suburbs where we can raise our own."

She covered her cheeks with her hands. "This can't be happening."

"Would you at least consider the idea of marrying me? I don't want to sound maudlin and say that I don't know how I'd get along without you in my life, but there it is. I know I'm not much of a catch. I'm impatient and irritable, I work too much, I don't know how to sit back and enjoy life. But you've shown me a whole new world out there, away from the office, and I'd like to learn more…with you as my teacher."

Dean watched her closely, wondering if he'd made a colossal mistake by coming to Phoenix to see her. She'd left everything she'd worked for in Chicago. Was it just to get away from him?

"Why did you leave?"

Some color had come back in her cheeks. Funny, but he'd never thought that his proposing marriage would cause a woman to almost faint.

"Because we can't seem to be together without ending up in bed."

"I'm afraid that's true. I have very little self-control where you're concerned." He took her hand once again. "I suppose that I've gone about all of this backward. Since it's the first time I've ever proposed, I'm not very good at it. The real question here is, do you love me?"

Her eyes filled with tears. He was such an idiot. The last thing he wanted was to make her cry.

She laced her fingers with his. "Yes, Dean, I'm in love with you despite everything I can do not to be."

"Is loving me so bad?"

"It is when you made it clear that you weren't interested in love."

"I was wrong. I can't think of a greater gift than you loving me."

The tears trickled down her face.

He cleared his throat. "As long as I'm already on my knees, I'd like to formally ask. Jodie Cameron, will you do me the great honor of marrying me, of loving me, of saving me from the horrible state of bachelorhood?"

She laughed through her tears. "Oh, Dean." She cupped his face in her hands. "If I'm dreaming, please don't wake me up."

"You can't be dreaming because my knees are killing me." He stood and held out his hand. "Well?"

She answered by throwing herself into his arms, covering his face with kisses.

After a lengthy and very passionate kiss, he pulled away long enough to say, "Is that a yes, by any chance?"

"Yes, Mr. Dean Logan, I will be most happy to marry you."

"And have a few children?"

"If that's what you want."

"That's very much what I want. Speaking of which—" he looked around the room "—where's your mother?"

"At work. She'll be home early this afternoon."

"I have an idea how we could spend our time waiting for her."

Yes, there was passion in his eyes, but Jodie saw something more, something she'd never expected to see—his eyes shining with love and tenderness. He had well and truly convinced her that he loved her. What more could she possibly want?

"Perhaps you'd like to show me what you have in mind," she replied.

With a shout of laughter he picked her up and carried her back down the hall to her bedroom.

He was right. He'd found the perfect way to spend the rest of the morning.

Epilogue

Six months later

"**Y**ou look like a princess in a fairy tale," her mother said to Jodie. She'd carefully placed the tiara and veil on Jodie's head while they stood before the large oval mirror in a room set aside for the bride.

Lynette added, "And who would have believed that Dean Logan would turn out to be a prince after all? If you'd told me a year or two ago that you would end up marrying Dean, I would have been convinced you were truly marrying an ogre."

"Lynette! Shame on you," her mother said. "Dean is a lovely man...polite, considerate and a joy to be around."

Jodie and Lynette shared a glance in the mirror and smiled at each other. Dean had done a great job of selling himself to their mom. Once Dean and Jodie had returned to Chicago, Jodie and Lynette had convulsed into laughter when Jodie had told Lynette about his visit to Phoenix.

"I've never attended a wedding this large, much less been in the wedding party," Mom said. "As you know, George and I eloped. And Chuck and Lynette had a small ceremony."

"Believe me, the idea of eloping ran through my mind many times these past few months," Jodie said. "I turned everything over to the wedding planner and went back to work."

"Dean said that since this would be his one and only wedding, he wanted a large celebration," Lynette explained. "He didn't care how much it cost. Everyone who's anyone in the business world was invited."

Jodie closed her eyes. She didn't need the reminder. She could see herself tripping down the aisle—literally tripping down the aisle—and skidding to a stop at Dean's feet.

There was a tap on the door. "Come in," she said.

Her three brothers, who were ushers, stepped inside. "Everyone's seated," Dave, the oldest, said.

Randy spoke up. "Wow, sis. You clean up pretty good."

"Gee, thanks, Randy. I'm glad you approve."

Rick, the impatient one, looked at his watch and said, "C'mon. Let's get this show on the road."

The three women followed the men out into the foyer. To save argument, both Kent and Kyle were ring bearers. Of course, that created an argument between them because each of them wanted to carry Jodie's ring. Lynette finally got that straightened out by threatening not to let them be a part of the wedding.

The music started and the young boys started down the aisle, looking sharp in their new suits. They were growing up so fast. Jodie blinked the moisture from her eyes. Get real. These are the same angelic beings who kept her constantly embarrassed with their frank questions to Dean every time they saw him.

Jodie had asked two of her coworkers to be bridesmaids. Lynette was her matron of honor and her mother would walk her down the aisle.

After Lynette reached the front of the church, the music switched to the well-known wedding march and the guests stood. Jodie's throat closed up. She was not going to cry, she was not going to cry, she was not—

Then she saw Dean waiting at the altar and that did it. Tears slid down her face as she started toward him. She couldn't stop smiling.

Jodie didn't remember much about the actual ceremony. She heard the rumble of Dean's voice and had responded when it was her turn, but all she could think about was the fact that she was actually marrying Dean Logan after all these months of answering the wedding planner's incessant questions.

"You may kiss the bride."

The pastor's words jolted her out of her reverie. Jodie turned to Dean, who was watching her with amusement. What? What did he find so amusing?

When he leaned toward her, he whispered, "I thought you were going to fall asleep there for a minute," and he kissed her.

He really kissed her. It wasn't a brushing of lips or a ritual peck on the mouth but a leisurely kiss. When he finally raised his head, her face was flaming and the guests were laughing and applauding.

Music filled the sanctuary as they started up the aisle. Once in the foyer, Dean turned to her. "Hello, Mrs. Logan. I hope you're having a good day."

"I wasn't going to fall asleep! I was just distracted a little."

"You must have been, since the pastor had to ask a couple of his questions to you twice."

"Oh, no." She covered her face with her hands. "And I didn't want to do anything to embarrass you. At least I didn't trip over the gown and fall down coming down the aisle!"

"You could never embarrass me, Jodie. I find you delightful, besides being the love of my life."

By now they were surrounded by well-wishers. After greeting several people, Dean and Jodie hurried outside and got into the limo waiting to take them to the large hotel where the reception would be held.

They settled into their seats, and Dean reached inside his coat pocket and pulled out a small, long and narrow box. "I want to give you your bride's gift before we get to the reception."

A necklace. He'd bought her a necklace. "Oh, Dean, what a thoughtful gift."

He lifted one eyebrow. "Aren't you going to open it?" he asked.

"Oh! I'm sure I'll love it," she said and lifted the lid.

There was no necklace. Only a folded envelope and a key. Bewildered, Jodie looked at him. He smiled.

She opened the envelope and found a note and two airline tickets to Hawaii. "Oh, we're going back to Hawaii!"

"Why not? That's where I really got to know you. This time we'll stay as long as you like."

She unfolded the note and read. "No, this isn't the key to my heart because you already have it in your safekeeping. This is a key to your new home."

"My home? What have you done?"

"Conspired behind your back. I got Lynette to go house hunting with me to find a home she thought you might like. Of course, if you don't like it, I can always—"

She threw herself into his arms and kissed him all over his face, his ears, his jaw and his mouth. "You are the most high-handed man I've ever known," she finally said, laughing with delight. "You bought me a house without consulting me?" She looked at him with mock disapproval, his face cupped in her hands.

"Actually I haven't bought it yet. I waited to sign the contract until you have a chance to see it. The Realtor gave me the key, and I thought we could go over there after we leave the reception. If you approve of it, I'll sign the papers before we leave."

So maybe a man could change a little. She was touched that he was trying. "I can hardly wait to see what you've picked out for us."

She knew that she would love the house because Lynette knew her so well. She would love it even more because Dean had chosen to surprise her with it.

One thing she knew for certain: there would never be a dull moment being married to Dean Logan.

* * * * *

From reader-favorite

Kathie DeNosky

THE ILLEGITIMATE HEIRS

A brand-new miniseries about three
brothers denied a father's name, but
granted a special inheritance.

Don't miss:

Engagement
between Enemies

(Silhouette Desire #1700,
on sale January 2006)

Reunion
of Revenge

(Silhouette Desire #1707,
on sale February 2006)

Betrothed
for the Baby

(Silhouette Desire #1712,
on sale March 2006)

WHAT HAPPENS IN VEGAS...

Shock! Proud casino owner
Hayden MacKenzie's former fiancée,
who had left him at the altar for a cool
one million dollars, was back in Sin City.
It was time for the lovely Shelby Paxton
to pay in full—starting with the wedding
night they never had....

His Wedding-Night Wager

by **Katherine Garbera**

On sale February 2006 (SD #1708)

Also look for:

Her High-Stakes Affair, March 2006
Their Million-Dollar Night, April 2006

COMING NEXT MONTH

#1705 TAKING CARE OF BUSINESS—Brenda Jackson
The Elliotts
How far will an Elliott heir go to convince a working-class woman that passion is color-blind?

#1706 TEMPT ME—Caroline Cross
Men of Steele
He is the hunter. She is his prey. And he's out to catch her at any cost.

#1707 REUNION OF REVENGE—Kathie DeNosky
The Illegitimate Heirs
Once run off the ranch, this millionaire now owns it…along with the woman who was nearly his undoing.

#1708 HIS WEDDING-NIGHT WAGER—
Katherine Garbera
What Happens in Vegas…
She left him standing at the altar. Now this jilted groom is hell-bent on having his revenge…and a wedding night!

#1709 SEVEN-YEAR SEDUCTION—Heidi Betts
Would one week together be enough to satisfy a seduction seven years in the making?

#1710 SURROGATE AND WIFE—Emily McKay
She was only supposed to have the baby…not *marry* the father of her surrogate child.

SDCNM0106